THE LEPER PRINCESS
AND
THE COURT JEW

by

Barak A. Bassman

TELEMACHUS PRESS

This book is a work of fiction. Names, characters, places and incidents are either the product of the author's imagination or are used fictitiously. Any resemblance to actual persons, living or dead, or to actual events or locales is entirely coincidental.

THE LEPER PRINCESS AND THE COURT JEW

Cover designed by Telemachus Press, LLC

Cover art:
Copyright © iStock/813207206_ilbusca

Published by Telemachus Press, LLC
http: //www.telemachuspress.com

ISBN: 978-1-945330-96-4 (eBook)
ISBN: 978-1-945330-98-8 (paperback)
ISBN: 978-1-945330-97-1 (hardback)

Library of Congress Location Number: 2017962535

FICTION / General
FICTION / Folklore

Version 2018.01.22

Table of Contents

THE LEPER PRINCESS
AND
THE COURT JEW

I. A Dead Man Walks the Earth

IT HAD HAPPENED during *Shabbat* services, on a Saturday morning, in the Great Synagogue in the *shtetl* of K____ in the land of Poland, that Zalman, who had carefully pretended to still be a living Jew, was exposed to the community as a walking corpse. Earlier that morning he had agreed to read the weekly Torah portion as the scheduled reader had fallen ill and lost his voice. Although it had been some time since Zalman had received such an honor, he did not spend much time weighing the wisdom of accepting it. To the contrary, he congratulated himself—silently—on how well he had fit into the society of the living.

The reading went well at first, as Zalman's Hebrew had always been strong, and he still recalled the basics of cantillation. Feeling emboldened, he let his fine baritone boom across the synagogue in celebration of the divine and wondrous Torah. But then four Hebrew letters cropped up in the scroll before him: *yod-heh-vav-heh*, the sacred name of the Holy One, Blessed be He. Zalman attempted to chant the word

Adonai—Lord—but no sound came forth. Disconcerted, he moved on quickly, hoping no one had noticed. They would not have noticed, he reassured himself, all the men were gossiping amongst themselves and ignoring the words of the Torah that *Shabbat* morning. Yet the name of the Holy One continually recurred in that weekly Torah portion and, each time, Zalman could not utter His Name.

There was one man paying close attention to Zalman's reading: the famed *Tzaddik* of K. _____, a *rebbe* renowned throughout Poland for his wisdom and learning. The *Tzaddik* famously meditated on each Hebrew letter in his prayers. And on *Shabbat* mornings, he blocked everything from his mind but the words Our Teacher Moses set down in the holy Torah and concentrated with all his soul on each syllable as it was chanted. His followers claimed he was able to harness the esoteric powers latent in the Hebrew letters to elevate himself into the upper realms, where he could plead his people's case directly before the Throne of Glory.

So when the *Tzaddik* sat that morning in his seat of honor by the Great Synagogue's Eastern Wall, he visibly directed his great powers of concentration upon Zalman's chanting. The *Tzaddik* eventually rose from his seat and demanded silence. The beadle obediently banged his stick hard against the reader's lectern and repeated the call for silence. The room fell quiet, the surprised men of K _____ turned their faces forward, and Zalman trailed off in his chanting. Once all eyes were on him, the *Tzaddik* pointed a bony forefinger at Zalman, and roared:

That man is an abomination!

That man, who is reading from our most holy Torah, is one of the dead, yet still somehow walking here in the daylight. Behold, he cannot pronounce the name of the Holy One, Blessed be He, which is the fount of all life and thus anathema to the dead.

The crowd converged around Zalman. The beadle picked up the silver *yad*, the pointer used by the Torah reader to track his place, found His Name in the scroll, and asked Zalman to pronounce the word. When he could not, the men gathered around him recoiled in terror, except for the *Tzaddik*.

There is nothing to fear, the *rebbe* told them, this is no demon. He is a hapless Jew who, for some reason, does not remain in his grave like a well-behaved corpse. We have to remedy this condition and free this poor soul to enter the World to Come. Come, take him to my home.

Two burly men in wrinkled, ill-fitting gabardines, whom, Zalman surmised, were looking for an excuse to leave the service anyway, escorted the dead man to the *Tzaddik*'s house. The saintly rabbi and his followers remained in the Great Synagogue to complete their *Shabbat* morning devotions.

These two burly men expressed no interest in their charge. Having carried this secret for so long—through countless decades, across so many towns and villages in Central and Eastern Europe—Zalman now felt an urge to unburden himself about what life was like when one is dead. All that was wanting was a politely awkward question to broach the subject.

But instead the two louts waddled through the main square of the *shtetl*, past the government building, the small church and a now empty tavern. The tavern-keeper's wife, a squat woman sweeping outside, yelled at the two lumbering dolts that they had still not paid their full tab from the night before. They cursed back at her in their slurred, faltering speech.

Zalman resigned himself to being the town drunks' excuse to nurse their hangovers in more hospitable places than the Great Synagogue. The things he could tell, if only they would care to hear: about how he had to pretend to eat when he did not actually need to eat at all. Or the long, boring nights when he had to pretend to need sleep like everyone else to avoid drawing suspicion.

Or how, as a dead man, it was imperative to avoid matrimonial entanglements. A by-product of death, even for the dead who managed still to be up and about, was an inability to perform basic conjugal duties. Truth be told, Zalman's lusts, the cause of so much anguish in his living years, had swiftly petered out once he became an animated corpse.

All this and more was he ready to tell at last. But one of the two oafs had just left their little procession, to go down a narrow side alley and discreetly vomit. The other stumbling lout took a sharp turn and dropped Zalman at the porch of the spacious villa belonging to the *Tzaddik*. The *rebbe*'s wife came outside and asked if prayers had ended so soon and if her husband and his followers were about to appear expecting a meal.

No, good lady, Zalman replied, they are still praying. Your husband asked me to come back here and wait for him. May I come in?

Of course, of course.

She showed Zalman into a chair in the front parlor and served him tea and honey cakes. He smiled, but did not touch the refreshments—no need to pretend anymore that he ate and drank like a living man. The thought of escaping briefly passed through his mind, starting over somewhere new and reprising his game of pretending to be alive. But what was the point? The *rebbe* was famous and would send word of the truth throughout the holy communities of the Jews in Europe and in the Turkish Empire.

Still, that weighing of risks and probabilities was not the real reason he had no desire to flee. Having been found out at last he was just too eager to tell some part of his long hidden story.

Soon enough, the *Tzaddik* and his followers returned home. The *Tzaddik* scolded his wife for wasting good food and drink on a dead man who did not need it and motioned for Zalman to follow him further back into the house. The *Tzaddik* only permitted three trusted followers to accompany them, telling the rest to wait, although they could help themselves to the tea and honey cakes.

Zalman followed him into his study. The *rebbe* sat down at his desk, rigidly upright and appearing ready to pronounce judgment. Thick red curtains covered the windows behind him, causing the sunlight to filter into the room as a blood-red mist that gave the *Tzaddik* the terrible visage of a harsh, avenging angel ready to denounce sinners before the Heavenly Tribunal in the World to Come. His three followers stood trembling in a corner near the door.

So, the *Tzaddik* began. How did this happen? Is this a punishment? Or has some witch or sorcerer worked an evil spell?

No, nothing of the sort, Zalman replied. My state was not commanded by the Name I can no longer utter or anyone else. The enchantment was my own doing.

But why? Death is nothing to fear. Our souls, our beautiful, immortal souls, break free from the limits of these gross husks and ascend to Paradise. It is not right for you to rove about the earth endlessly in this unnatural state. You are exhausted from the strain. I can see that plainly. Tell me the enchantment you worked, and I will undo it. I promise we will bury you here with great honor in the Jewish cemetery, and that I personally will say *Kaddish* for your soul. Let go of this ceaseless wandering. Truth, His Holy and Perfect Truth, awaits you in the upper realms.

Zalman shook his head and laughed bitterly.

No, *Rebbe*, I am afraid your wisdom falls short here. I have good reason to fear the next world. My soul is black, and my deeds are foul. Nothing awaits me but fiery, scalding lashes from cackling demons with scaly skin and flicking serpents' tongues. I have lived this way, that is, lived as a dead man, far longer than my true human lifespan could ever have been. This enchantment has kept me safe.

How great can your sins be? Do you think so highly of yourself that you alone of His children have reached some pinnacle of wickedness that will awe the Heavenly Tribunal? He saw His children err during the generation before the Flood. He saw the wicked in Sodom and Gomorrah. He watched whores and idolaters pollute His Holy Temple in

Jerusalem. Are you so mighty and terrible that your crimes truly stand out against these? Do not flatter yourself. The gates of repentance are always open to an ordinary sinning Jew, and I am sure you are no more and no less than that.

Zalman shook his head once more.

You may convince the cowering fools who flock to your court that you have special knowledge of things that are hidden, but I have walked the earth far longer than one lifetime and I have seen more and I know more. I have seen the avenging angels sharpening their blades and drooling in anticipation at the sight of me, sniffing me as their prey. I have spoken to wandering spirits from the other side who have told me what my fate will be. Your words are childish.

The *Tzaddik*'s face narrowed in a scowl, and he tightly gripped the desk's edge. His old, taut body quivered beneath his elegant silk gabardine.

You arrogant fool, the *rebbe* hissed, you dare, and in my own house, to challenge my authority and my ability to intercede in the upper realms?

Zalman was growing bored with this conversation, and regretted not escaping to another town. The avenging angels and the raging demons with their instruments of torture awaiting his soul filled him with genuine terror, but he had long ceased to get exercised over the wailing of mortal men. He no longer felt pain, in his body or in his spirit, from the acts of ordinary human beings, and this tiresome petty sage with his prickly self-regard was no exception. Still, it was always simpler to avoid unnecessary confrontation that only made life—or this post-life wandering—more bothersome. So Zalman decided to appease the old rabbi.

I do not mean to challenge your authority or question your ability to intercede upon behalf of your community or your followers. But my case is different. The judgment was written upon my soul before your birth. There is nothing you can do. If I had any reason to hope, then I would gladly put my trust in you and your piety and your learning.

The *Tzaddik* calmed down. He paused, looked up to the ceiling, mumbled something Zalman did not catch, and then, after another pause, looked back at his dead-but-not-quite guest.

Perhaps I can help you. I believe you when you say you have sinned greatly. And instead of repenting you have chosen to hide, like Jonah fleeing the Holy One's command and sailing to Tarshish. You can no longer seek forgiveness from those whom you have wronged, because they are properly dead. So you fear even more and hide even more. I understand you are an exceptional case. That is why you need my guidance. If you tell me your tale, and if you truly repent, I can advocate on your behalf before the Throne of Glory in the World to Come.

After all, what do you have to lose? If I cannot help you after learning your tale, then you can try to keep going the way you have been. But whatever enchantment you are using will one day fail you. The magic will wear off, the way the sole of a shoe wears away from walking on it day after day, or in a moment of weakness you will falter somehow and lack the strength to continue hauling about your dried up, rotted husk of a body.

And what happens then? The wrath of the Holy One and His angels shall be beyond all measure. You will have enraged them through your arrogant conviction that you alone may escape righteous judgment. Nor will you have any repentance to point to in your defense, or any sage to plead your cause.

But the Holy One, Blessed be He, does not wish to harm His children of Israel. That is why, unable to penetrate your hard heart any other way, He sent you to me. This is your opportunity to be relieved of your terrible burden and to repent your sins. You may not receive another chance.

Zalman pondered the *Tzaddik*'s words. He was confident in the potency of his magic, which had proved durable over so many decades. But perhaps the *rebbe* was right—he supposed he could not evade judgment forever. And what was the worst that would come from confiding in this old man? Without Zalman's cooperation, the spell could not be lifted, and his dead body was incapable of feeling pain. All the old man could do would be to shunt him along to the next wretched little town.

Fine, I will tell my tale. But your followers must leave. You and I will sit alone, no interruptions until I have finished.

The *Tzaddik* agreed, and his followers quietly exited. Once the door closed behind them, and their footsteps faded in the distance, Zalman began.

II. A Happy Childhood in the Abundant Household of the Court Jew

I GREW UP a long time ago, to the west and to the south of this area, in the Duchy of W______. I do not believe this Duchy exists anymore. The last Duke lost his lands fighting the Turks, or maybe it was the Austrians. But at the time of my birth, it was a beautiful, flourishing place.

The Duchy was nestled in the mountains, and interspersed with fertile valleys. The Duke lived in a series of small castles and forts embedded into the sides of different mountains, a ploy by his ancestors to guarantee the high ground in case of attack. Within the walls of his castles, the Duke lived a life befitting a prince. There were great halls where he and his retainers gorged themselves on the finest delicacies and wines. Traveling poets entertained them with songs of famous Gentile knights fighting monsters or questing after relics of their holy men. The walls were hung with tapestries showing brutal men hunting magical beasts in sunny forests.

The Duke and the Duchess were as different as a husband and a wife could be. The Duchess had been born far away. Alone in a strange land she cleaved to the priests and to the church for comfort. The Gentiles considered her to be very pious.

The Duke was a man of worldly appetites. He loved to spend his days riding through his mountain forests hunting game, before indulging in drink at night. His wife stormed out in disgust from his orgies of gluttony; so he took to keeping a stable of mistresses.

I see you shaking your head in shame, *Rebbe*. These were indeed sinful people. But where am I, you ask, and where are the Jews? What do these drunken Gentiles and their coarse ways have to do with His holy community of Israel?

As in many such German princedoms in those bygone days, there were scattered Jewish communities, each eking out meager livings in between the great lords and their sharp pointed lances above, and the miserable, bitterly envious serfs below. Clusters of Jews lived here and there in villages in the countryside, artisans mostly, cobblers, blacksmiths and so on. Some villages could barely muster a *minyan*. They were poor and not very learned, but these Jews held steadfast to the Torah as best they could and waited humbly and patiently for the Messiah to come rescue them from the sufferings of their exile.

My father was not one of these humble Jews. My father, may his memory be a blessing, was a great merchant. He had grown up in a neighboring duchy and been brought to W____ at the Duke's behest. The Duke needed a wealthy merchant to loan him money, to collect his taxes, to trade his surplus grain harvest and to manage his treasury. All this and more my father did for him. With my father's wise guidance, the Duke's wealth swelled ever larger, freeing him to indulge his various and sundry carnal desires.

My father used his influence at court to secure the safety of the Duke's Jews. If, as sometimes happened, the priest in a village incited terrible hatred and violence towards the Jews in his Easter sermon, my father had obtained the Duke's agreement to give sanctuary to the Jews in his fortresses until the trouble subsided.

My father was also the most learned Jew in the duchy. When he was a young man he had studied in a famed *yeshiva* in Germany. As a small boy I remember waking to the sound of him chanting a page of Talmud. He would answer questions about the Torah put to him by the village Jews, and he paid, out of his pocket, for the *cheders* to operate in the villages, so that the sons of the Jewish artisans could read and write and know something of the Torah and the wisdom of our holy sages of blessed memory.

He was a good man, my father. A righteous man, a pillar of his generation. I was his only son—after me there were only daughters—and I was the joy of my father's life. The best tutors, the most brilliant young men from the most august *yeshivot* of Germany, came to teach me in our home and to live with us. We lived in a manor house near the Duke's favorite castle, where there was a whole wing set aside for me and my tutors. We would prop up our books on silken cushions as we studied and debated the words of the holy sages.

I have never known more grateful men than those tutors. After years of sleeping on wooden benches in drafty synagogues and begging meals from local townspeople, they now slept on soft beds and filled their bellies every night with roasted meat and fragrant wine. Their faces were always so full of sadness when they left us to get married and move in with their new fathers-in-law.

During my childhood I was all that my father could have hoped. My life revolved around the holy Torah, and I spent my days doing little but studying. My mother or my sisters would bring me food and drink to keep my body and soul stitched together, but they dared not disturb me in my holy labor. I was feted and admired throughout our household.

Once my grandfather visited, my mother's father, and he tested my knowledge of the Talmud at length. After I had answered all his questions and quoted many long passages from memory, my mother burst into tears of joy. She offered prayers of thanksgiving for being blessed with such a son. My childish head swelled with pride.

My father was often away. He had to attend to His Excellency when the Duke traveled about the princedom or, every now and then, to another principality. Sometimes my father had to make the rounds of the villages flanked by armed knights, to ensure the proper collection of taxes. Or he had to meet with other great merchants in distant cities.

I bitterly resented my father's absences. Mother was kind, yet she shook with holy awe in my presence. And she did not understand my struggles with the holy texts. But father, he was a comfort and a guide to me. He was a tall man, powerfully built, with a thick black beard. I would sit on his wide, warm lap and talk of my studies and questions and theories of interpretation until I fell asleep in his arms. He always listened to me so patiently, always gently steered me to the right text, to the right interpretation. Each night before bed he kissed me tenderly on the forehead, a hot, wet kiss that I thought was the very essence of the love of Israel's Father for His children.

I had no idea then, being only a foolish, selfish boy, how many cares wore my poor father down. For despite his many merits, he had many enemies. The peasants in the villages hated him because the Duke sent my father to collect their taxes. The priests, of course, only encouraged this hatred.

But this was nothing compared to the venom of the Duchess. She hated how my father's shrewd management of the Duke's estates allowed him the freedom to indulge his terrible appetites. And her confessor was always whispering that her husband ill-treated her and fornicated and sinned because of the malevolent influence of the Jews. She and her priests were always plotting my father's downfall. It was only the abundant goodness and honesty of his soul, which was clear to the Duke and the Duke's closest knights and that kept him safe.

I saw little of other children when I was a boy. My sisters were too terrified to play with me, since my mother would explode in a towering rage if they tried to disturb my studies—the brilliant young scholar, the family's prodigy, must be left alone with the holy books.

Sometimes Jewish boys from the nearby villages came around, usually on some errand—passing along a request to my father, or delivering shoes, or meat, or whatnot. I rarely saw the village boys on these visits. Yet every so often we would cross paths by accident—mother would tell some village boy to wait in the kitchen, and I would bump into him as I went for a quick snack.

I found it hard to speak with the village boys. They were so dirty, and they spoke in a coarse, ugly slang I could not follow. I lived in a magical universe of holy sages debating the most profound questions of Torah and of the beautiful tales of the *Aggadah*. I would speak to them in my singsong dreamy voice, expressing my sentiments in parable, or through stringing quotations together from the holy books. But village boys could not follow my mix of Hebrew, Aramaic, and the High German of the Duke's Court (for that was the German we spoke in our household). Some boys, not sure what to do, laughed nervously. Some boys nodded politely and looked away. None of them would answer me back.

I grew to hate them. In the arrogance of my youth, I scorned them as illiterate savages, unfit for the blessing of being members of the holy community of Israel, of His Chosen People who alone were gifted with the Torah. I delighted in cleverly insulting them through choice quotations they could not understand.

Yet I felt sad if a long time passed without a village boy visiting our kitchen. I hated them through and through, but I was inconsolable if they were not there for me to hate.

What is that, *rebbe*? You think I felt some instinctive love of the people of Israel? I doubt that was the case. I never wanted friends when I was a boy. I loved only myself then and was intoxicated with my own genius. I yearned for the other boys not out of love, but out of an urge to be adored and honored.

I see you are shaking your head. I know you are right. Studying Torah for one's own glorification and one's own ability to ridicule others is sinful. Yes, now that I have lived more than one full lifetime, I know this too. But back then, I knew so much and so little all at once. What could I do? I was lauded and pampered by everyone around me and took these indulgences not as gifts, but as the inevitable and just reward of my own merits.

After my *bar mitzvah*, my father decided to teach me about the world and about business. He taught me how to figure interest and profits on loans, how to assess collateral, what to buy and how and when to sell it. We traveled together all across the Duchy and to foreign lands when the Duke requested or when we needed the aid of other great Jewish merchants.

Those were exciting days. Everything was new: the feeling of being on the road, riding in a carriage, the smell of wooden tables and thick soup in a country inn, the thrill of matching our wits and stratagems against rival merchants. Now, when everything feels so stale and worn to me after centuries of wandering, those days of anticipation and glee flicker dimly in my memory, and fill me with longing.

And my father, what a *mensch*! He never became upset, never raised his voice, no matter what happened—when passing monks spat upon him as a greedy dirty Jew, or when other merchants tried to cheat him or accuse him of cheating them, or when a carriage would break down and we would be stranded in the forest for hours without proper food and drink, still he was always serene. He would sigh and tell me to trust in the workings of Him Whose Name I can no longer utter. Everything will work itself out, he would assure me, and if we should suffer a little here and little there, well, we are cleansing ourselves of some sin in this world so that we can more easily enjoy the delights of the World to Come.

Nor did my father ever slacken in his devotion to Torah. On our trips, I always woke to the sight of my father wrapped in his *tefillin*, joyously, sometimes tearfully, reciting his prayers. And he always traveled with whatever tractate of the Talmud he was studying.

I see from your broad smile that you admire my father. As do I. The finest man I have ever known.

My father was not only training me to be as accomplished a merchant as I already was a scholar, but he also knew that I was a young man without a wife, and it was his sacred duty to fix that deficiency. So our business trips often doubled as matchmaking trips. We would visit with the wealthiest Jews in Central Europe, distinguished merchants like my father. In the beginning everything was business, my father and the other merchant hashing out whatever it was they hashed out and bargaining over whatever it was they bargained over. I kept careful notes of what was agreed, but was under strict instructions not to interfere.

At some point this struggle of wills would end. Then brandy would be poured and toasts raised. A bit into the drinking my father would broach some thorny problem of Torah, about which he would feign perplexity.

That was my cue. I would then launch into a display of my learning to prove what an excellent prospective son-in-law I was. A scholar! A prodigy! A genius! No dowry could be too great for me! No girl's beauty could merit such learning! Or so I told myself after showing off my subtle reasoning.

Most of the time the half-drunk merchant host would sit back, pretend to follow my discourse and be suitably impressed. Every so often we came across a merchant who was himself an able scholar, and he would test me with problems of even greater complexity. But my learning always pulled me through.

My father, having shown his wares, waited for the other merchant to show off his, that is, his daughters. Some excuse would carry us into the dining room of our host's villa, where his daughters would parade in front of me, serving us delicacies and pouring yet more brandy. The girls would show off something they had recently sewn. Or present us with honey cakes they had baked. My father would question these girls on the most minute details of household management—how much to pay servants, how to tell if a servant was stealing, how to tell a good piece of meat, how to keep a kosher home and on and on. The poor girls, he poked and prodded them like a suspect shipment of grain.

I was too embarrassed to ask them questions, so I blushed and looked away. What did I know then? Women were horrible tempters, demons, they were Lilith. *Rebbe*, do you recall the tale of the holy sage, may his memory be for a blessing, who burned out his eyes with red hot nails so he would not be tempted by the sight of women into neglecting the study of the Torah? They terrified me. I felt my soul was at stake as one of them would no doubt try to lure me into committing an awful, unpardonable sin.

But eventually I peeked at them. And what did I see? No Lilith, no sultry demonic temptresses, just awkward nervous girls trying not to do anything that would upset their fathers.

Having looked into their eyes and seen only stammering modesty, I held them in contempt. Real women, powerful women, I told myself, were the confident demon seductresses, but these were pitiful, scared little girls. I delighted in launching into learned discourses in their presence that they could not follow, only so I could watch them fidget and breathe carefully and try to react appropriately to whatever I was intoning in half-Aramaic.

Needless to say, none of these girls struck my fancy in the slightest. After a while, my father tried to nudge me towards a match. Miriam, he would say, the fine daughter of such and such whom we had met, she would make an excellent wife. If you wish, just say the word, I can work out the dowry and the betrothal terms.

But I felt no desire for Miriam. In my fevered, lustful dreams, the kind hot-blooded young men have, I saw tall, arrogant demons, with waves of sweetly perfumed black hair and swiveling hips and smirking blood-stained lips. How could Miriam compare? There she sat, with her pale skin covered in pimples, with her sallow cheeks, with her terrified eyes constantly darting over to her drunken father for reassurance she was not making a fool of herself and him, too.

So I would make up some excuse. I thought the girl looked sickly, or she seemed to be confused on some point of *kashrut*, or her family lived too far away. My father sighed. He knew I was lying, but he could not fathom why. Still, he would say to me, when the match is right, when it is the match ordained by the Heavenly Court, you will know, and it will all happen as it should happen. I too, my father would say, went through a stage when the daughters of Israel could not satisfy me. But, when I saw your mother, so kindly, so modest, so pious, I knew she was a blessing sent to me from the higher realms.

I would nod absent-mindedly through these speeches. But I could not imagine warming myself in a bed with some squealing, trembling pious little mouse.

I see the rage boiling in your eyes now, *Rebbe*. Starting to believe that I have sins to answer for before the Throne of Glory? *Nu*, this is nothing. These are the idle sins of a dreamy arrogant boy. As I had no interest in modest Jewish girls, yearning instead in my filth-ridden dreams for a beautiful demon princess even more arrogant than I was, the demon king Samael smelled his prey and decided to make sport of me.

III. The Princess with the Golden Hair

IT WAS A Christian girl, a *shikse*, who brought me low. Who was she and how did my pious father let me near her? This was no servant girl with loose morals. If anything, the girl's morals were stricter than even the most pious Jewish maiden.

Her name was Carolina, and she was the Duke's eldest daughter. She was the most beautiful woman I had ever seen, far more lovely than Rachel by the well or Bathsheba tempting David. This princess was about my age—a little older, a little younger, it is hard to recall, it was so long ago, but it does not really matter, just about—and she was in the prime of her life. She was tall, tall as the Duke himself, and she had the most wondrous long, perfectly combed golden hair. She was pale, and her eyes often drifted heavenward. An angel, the Christians at the Duke's court would say.

The Duke had little interest in his daughters. And why should he? Daughters could not go hunting. And a pious saintly girl only made the Duke feel remorse when taking his pleasures. Still, His Excellency was no fool, and he took note of his good fortune in having a daughter so beautiful and so pious that no one would ever cast aspersions on her virginity. This daughter was rare goods, and her father meant to cash her in for all he could get. My father was one of the Duke's advisors in these machinations, plotting which princely marriage alliance would be most advantageous. Who knew, with a girl like that, even the Holy Roman Emperor himself was not out of the question.

But I see you are getting impatient. What does the *Tzaddik* sitting with me here, now, care about the matchmaking intrigues of long-dead *goyim*? You are here for a Jew's holy soul, and you want to know what these matters have to do with this Jew and his soul. Well, as I said, my father was grooming me to be a merchant and bringing me into all his business dealings. And the center of those dealings was the Duke. So it was imperative that I be introduced at the Duke's court, and make friends and alliances there.

My father waited a full year and a half after my *bar mitzvah* before he let me set foot in the Duke's court. There would be no rescuing me if I made an ill impression, and he had to be sure I was ready. I still remember my excitement when my father told me my time to enter court society had at last come. The Duke was returning from a hunting trip in three days' time, my father told me, and he wanted to discuss all his financial affairs. I was to accompany my father to counsel the Duke and his closest companions.

My father gave me clear instructions on how to behave: Never speak unless spoken to—the presence of Jews at court was barely tolerated, and they expected their Jews to say no more than necessary. Show great honor to every Christian, even boors with far less learning and wealth than you. There is no point in humiliating a boor at the Duke's court—he will just become an enemy who will spread poisonous lies about the Jews and who could ultimately, may it never happen in our lifetime, turn the Duke against us. Other princes had grown angry with their court Jews, cut off their heads, seized their wealth and exiled whatever other Jews were left in their domains. Who could know if today's ignorant boor would someday become the Duke's bosom comrade?

And then there was the matter of food. I simply assumed we would eat and drink nothing—how could anything prepared in the Duke's kitchen be kosher? Don't be silly, my father said, we will be staying over as the Duke's guests. Do you think we will be fasting the whole time? With nothing in your belly and your throat parched, do you think you can keep the Duke's tax receipts and loans and assets from swimming in your mind? Of course not. So my father told me, don't eat pork and avoid any dairy dishes so as not to mix meat and milk, as these were prohibitions the Duke knew and respected. But he would take it quite amiss if we ate nothing. How could filthy Jews be so arrogant as to look down upon the delicacies at His Excellency's table!

It was especially important to eat the venison cut from the carcasses of those cloven-hooved beasts. If the Duke had killed fine deer during his hunt, he expected his companions—including his Jew—to rejoice heartily and to praise the quality of the meat. The Duke cared more about honor being shown to the roasted venison than to his despised shrew of a Duchess.

I was aghast. To hear such words from any Jew would have sickened me, but from my father, who was so pious, who guided unlearned village Jews in *kashrut*? How could this be? I see from your face, *Rebbe*, that you too are horrified at my father's words.

I assaulted my father with the wisdom of our holy sages. I quoted the *halakhah*, the law, on food that is prohibited, and I reminded him of our noble ancestors and their great suffering. Had the saintly Rabbi Akiba martyred himself to the wicked Romans rather than abandon his love for Torah only so my father could shrug off the commandments to flatter the Duke's vanity in overpowering some poor frightened animal in the forest?

My father laughed at me. Silly child. Do you pay attention to the *Megillah* reading on *Purim*? he asked me. Of course, I replied. Then, my father continued, you know well how Esther was able to use her position at the King of Persia's court to foil the plans of Haman and thereby save the lives of untold thousands of Jews. Of course I know all that, I replied.

My father continued: When Esther was seducing the King with all her charms, did she keep strictly kosher? When the King wanted to recline his head into her bosom and to feed her delicacies, like a gallant lover, did Esther lecture her husband on the finer points of what foods the Torah deems forbidden? If she had, the King's ardor would have cooled, and his affection for Esther would have faded away. Our now pious kosher Queen Esther would have been helpless to defeat Haman's plans and the Jews of Persia would have been butchered and their property looted.

Don't think there are no Hamans at the Duke's court. The priests who surround the Duchess and feed on her sorrow and bitterness, they whisper into Her Ladyship's ear all about the Jews. The Duke's sins, they say, are caused by the evil presence of the Jews. Just kill the Jews, or exile them and confiscate their property for the Church, and you will be happy again. Your husband will love you and will devote himself to living an exemplary life of Christian morality.

And what stops these vipers? The esteem the Duke bears for me, just as the love of King Ahasuerus for Esther stopped Haman. Like Esther, I bend the Torah a little when I need to, but I do so to safeguard the lives and possessions of the scattered remnants of Israel. Until the Messiah should come—may it be speedily and in our days, *amen selah*—we must rely on the generosity and sufferance of our Christian lords.

And one last thing, my father said: Never look at their women. No matter how splendidly attired they may be, no matter how they dazzle with sweet perfumes and flowing hair, to be entangled with their women will leave you only the options of conversion (to wed her), exile (if the Duke is merciful), or death (if the Duke feels a point is to be made).

In the nights before I was to enter the Duke's presence I slept poorly. I was terrified of these great lords, and of the necessity of sinning to protect the holy community of Jews in the Duchy—to have the strength to walk in the footsteps of Queen Esther. I would wake from terrible nightmares, breathing hard. I would fall to my knees, tears streaming down and pray for wisdom. My father, whose room was next to mine, snored like a fat contented ox.

The morning we set out was cold and windy. My father and I donned our finest garments, gabardines of lovely silk, and ordered a carriage to bring us to the castle. We moved slowly, as the wind lashed hard against the horses. The coachman cursed and moaned. I took these as ill omens and prayed fervently. My father ignored me and the foul wind, instead poring over his records of the Duke's tax collections. When he came upon an entry he could not follow, he asked me to explain it. But I was too busy praying to hear him.

A hard smack went right to the side of my head. The question was repeated, and I answered it. The entry in the ledger had been mine.

Good, my father said, the Duke will have no patience for a sniveling, terrified boy. Be strong, be calm, have faith in our Creator and our Shepherd that His will shall be carried out and His might shall protect us.

When we arrived at the castle, the drawbridge was lowered, and we made our way over the moat and past the fortress walls. I shuddered at the sight of so many men idling about with swords, some knights in full armor, some squires stumbling about half awake. My flesh suddenly seemed so fragile, and a gust of that biting hard wind could hurl any of those swords through my soft unprotected belly.

My father led me to a nearby keep, and we mounted the stone steps. The various passersby—knights, priests, noblemen—they all knew my father and greeted him as a dear, long lost friend. I was introduced as his son, a fine young man. My terror turned to pride: My father was a great man among the other grandees of the Duchy. What other Jews could walk so brazenly into the Duke's castle and be welcomed with such honor?

We approached two immense wooden doors, over which hung the ducal coat of arms. My father bowed to the steward stationed outside and asked: Is His Excellency ready to receive us? We have brought, as requested, all of the tax ledgers.

The steward motioned us in. We entered a spacious hall hung with bright tapestries, all showing princes and knights killing different beasts in the forest, even a white unicorn. There was a table set with pastries and a jug of wine, at the end of which sat the Duke himself. He was the biggest man I had ever seen, wide as he was tall, with fire red hair and red beard both falling below his shoulders and covered in layers of robes made from the hides of animals he had killed. A sword in a jewel-encrusted scabbard hung loosely at his side. The Duke smelled of sweat and drink. His companions were equally sweaty, but much shorter and less imposing. Still, they all had such hard, brutal faces—the faces of men whose natural way is to kill for sport in the forest.

My father humbly greeted the Duke and introduced me. The Duke grunted his greetings in return and directed us to sit. He wasted no time, but immediately demanded to know the precise state of his tax revenues. My father opened the ledger and meticulously explained everything to His Excellency. I was too terrified to speak, but it did not matter because my father handled the entire discussion.

The Duke visibly relaxed. Whatever had been bothering him was soothed by my father's careful books and accounts. Cups were filled with wine, a toast was raised and all drank

joyously to His Excellency's health, my father and I too. The
Duke asked after my mother and the news of the Duchy's
Jewish community. He asked what my father had heard might
have been brewing in a neighboring principality, where he
knew my father had well-placed friends and relations. He
even asked whether my father had found a wife yet for me. I
blushed deeply, and all the bearded men laughed.

The Duke ordered a servant to make up a guest room
for us, and invited us to a feast that night. Which we of
course accepted most graciously and humbly.

Once we were alone again, settled in the guest room, my
father lay down and slept. But I could not rest. I looked out
the window: Everywhere I gazed I saw the Duke's men,
armed men, stewards, servants, cooks, everyone bustling
about. I tried to look away, beyond the castle, but the high
ramparts blocked my view. We were trapped in this dangerous place, surrounded by so many Christian swords. I
wrapped my *tefillin* upon my arm and my head and prayed. I
do not even know what I prayed for. I think I prayed because
the sight and sound of Hebrew words comforted me.

After what seemed an eternity we were summoned to
eat. And what a feast! You have not seen a feast until you
have been to the table of a great nobleman like that Duke.
We entered a vast hall, even larger than the other rooms I had
seen. The walls were covered again in boldly colored tapestries celebrating the hunting and killing of all sorts of animals.

There was a huge table, shaped like a horseshoe, which
ran the length of the room. At the head sat the Duke, his
sons and his bosom companions. My father and I were seated
discreetly far away on one side. Every so often the Duke

would summon my father to discuss some point or other, but, for the most part, His Excellency felt it prudent not to make too much of a public display of his friendship for the Jews.

The evening's entertainers performed in the center of the horseshoe. There was a poet, I recall, a swarthy fellow from somewhere far away. He spoke German passably, but in a thick accent. He sang to us of knights tramping about England in search of a magic cup, which their Jesus had somehow deposited a thousand miles from his home in Jerusalem. The whole stupid thing made no sense to me, and I longed for the sweet words of our holy sages.

I am glad to have finally pulled another approving look from your face, *Rebbe*. I was worried that you had already given me up for damned, before I had even told you my truly horrendous sins.

But alas I had no Talmud tractate or book of Midrash with me, so I distracted myself by looking around. As I said, we were seated far from the Duke, way down the side of the horseshoe table. We were surrounded by the Duchess and her entourage, as the Duke wanted them also far away from him and his companions, and, besides, he knew Her Ladyship would take particular offense at being seated near Jews. The Duchess sat there tightly scowling. She made a point of eating nothing her husband had killed in his hunt, but only bread and water. She would not look at me or my father.

She was surrounded by a group of Christian priests—mad, hard fanatics. Their lined faces and thin lips never stopped mumbling prayers and curses. Their eyes stared at me in icy rage. At first I tried to smile back at them in order to extend honor and gratitude. This only seemed to make them shake with yet more fury. So I decided to move my eyes elsewhere.

And thus my eyes wandered to another member of the Duchess's party: Carolina, the Duke's daughter. Her face looked that night like a radiant moon rising above the dirt and soot around her, a crescent moon—long, a little curved and so lovely—pale and glowing. I found myself looking at her more than I should, but there was such tenderness in her eyes, grey and sad and understanding. If she were a Jew, I would have said the radiance of the *Shekhinah* shone out from within her.

She noticed my staring. But Carolina did not, as I feared, reprimand me in any way. Far from it, she summoned me to approach her seat and engaged me in polite conversation. Was I my father's son, she asked? Was this my first time at court? What did Jewish boys do and learn as they grew up? She seldom had the chance to speak to a Jew, so she was very curious about our habits—what we ate, how we dressed, all our different holidays.

I answered as best I could. It was as if a serpent had lodged in my throat and was trying to strangle my words. But I did not fear her worldly position. No, that could have been excused and explained. I had begun my true descent into hideous sin. I felt the fear that a lover feels when faced with his beloved, the fear that any wrong word will anger her and drive her away forevermore.

I see your eyes, *Rebbe*, narrowing in rage. Pace yourself, my good saint, there is far worse to come.

Just as your eyes narrow now, so did the priests' eyes dart angrily at Carolina. It would not do for their charge to be chattering away with a filthy, conniving Jew. The Duchess wanted her reared with the strictest bile against the Jewish people.. So they tried to interject and put a stop to our discussion. But Carolina would brook no interference. She reminded her confessors that this was a festive occasion, and I was her family's guest.

That night, after the meal, my father and I retired back to the same bedroom in the castle. I lay down on a cot, and began to drift away happily into sleep. Each star shining into the window seemed to twinkle in joyous love of the Princess Carolina, the benefactress of all things bright and heavenly. I had no idea what I wanted to do, other than to sit at her feet and to look up into those grey eyes.

My father was now the restless one. What did you think you were doing? he hissed at me. Their women are vipers. Stay away. If the Duke thinks you have impure thoughts for his daughter, your life will be worth precious little. I should have foisted a Jewish wife on you before now, so you could cool that ardent blood with a proper bride. That girl's reputation for virginity is worth a great deal to the Duke. There are negotiations, quite sensitive; they plan to use her for a marriage alliance with certain powerful noble houses.

I promised my father not to speak to the Princess again, and I apologized for my rash behavior. My contrition was genuine: I was terrified that I may have stupidly done something to imperil my father and by extension all the Jews of the Duchy. The Holy One had entrusted the care of His flock in

                    Barak A. Bassman

the Duchy to us, and my *yetzer hara*, my evil inclination, had led me down a dangerous path. I recognized my silly joy to be nothing but the snare of Ashmedai and his demons, out to corrupt the hearts of the sons of Israel. That night I prayed for forgiveness while my father slept.

And that should have been the end of the matter. A brief indiscretion, a stumble towards sin, which would not be repeated. But fate, or more specifically, the Duke, would have it otherwise. As I learned in time, the Duchess had hurled bitter reproaches at the Duke about his impertinent Jews daring to make idle chatter with the Princess Carolina, poisoning her pure soul with their wicked ways and lies. The Duke was delighted—he had found a wonderful new way to poke the shrew he loathed so deeply.

So thus I found myself a frequent guest at the Duke's table, always seated right next to the Princess, and across from the Duchess. My worried father sat on my other side, helplessly watching the spectacle unfold. As much as my father yearned for me to break off all relations with Carolina—he saw nothing but ill omens there—he also feared angering the Duke by ruining His Excellency's new favorite sport with the hated Duchess.

I was—and I know you will be disgusted with my behavior, *Rebbe*, but I have promised a full and forthright confession—I was spinning with delight. To be in the presence of the Princess delighted my senses—the long golden hair, the sweet smell of her perfume, the way her bosom heaved gently up and down when she yawned. When I was away from her, reading about our mother Sarah or our mother Rachel, may their memories be for a blessing, I pictured Carolina walking in ancient Israel. My mind could no longer stay focused on a page of Talmud. To me, everything was the Princess.

Now you may be wondering: What does a Jewish boy discuss with a *shikse* Princess? The Princess was very devout. If I spent all my time thinking of her, she spent all her time thinking of Jesus and Mary. She had no interest in the politics of the Duchy, and she would sigh slowly, like a candle sputtering, whenever talk turned to her possible marriage to some grand nobleman or other.

But just discuss matters of heaven, and then her cheeks brightened like ripe apples and her voice became quick and joyful. Being so desperate to please her, I indulged her desire to speak of otherworldly matters. Oftentimes the Princess spoke at length about the travails of this Christian saint or that one about whom she had been reading. She especially loved tales of Christian women who were martyred because they defended their chastity. She somehow never tired of stories of lovely, pious girls killing themselves, or inviting death from others, rather than submit to a man's carnal lusts.

Occasionally she would ask me questions about Jewish laws or customs. She seemed genuinely baffled that our holy sages had not recognized the truth of Christianity and kept asking if, somewhere in all those Hebrew and Aramaic books I had read, there was some acknowledgement of the tenets of her faith. Each time I told her no, of course not, she would turn those sad, grey eyes upon her lap and mumble something under her breath in Latin.

While my father was powerless to stop me from seeing the Princess at official feasts, he did try to turn my eyes in other directions. My father was a clever man—he could not have survived so long at the Duke's court otherwise—and he noticed that I was led astray by my eyes, and how alluring they found the female form. This was how the Evil One was tempting me. So my father decided to use the same tactic to lure me back into a life of righteousness. Or so he hoped.

His matchmaking efforts intensified. But there were no more discussions of dowries and business alliances. No, the matchmakers were given but one instruction: find the most beautiful maiden in Ashkenaz, even if she were the destitute orphan of a manual laborer with no learning or pedigree. No dowry required—you see how I drove my father to desperation, I, the learned son, the prodigy son of a great and powerful merchant, was to be married without a dowry! And why? Because my father was convinced that only a physical beauty greater than Carolina's could lure me back towards the holy community of Israel.

So the matchmakers scoured the duchies and principalities of the Holy Roman Empire until they found Zipporah. She came from a village where her father, a failed tailor, had become the disgrace of the Jews, a drunkard worse than the worst of the *goyim*. But his Zipporah, his eldest daughter, was an outstanding beauty: a tall girl, with thick blue-black hair and intense, angry black eyes. You would think this lout would be overjoyed at such a match for his daughter, especially with no dowry needed. But no, he insisted my father pay *him*. And my father was so worried about my dalliances with the Princess that he actually agreed. Thanks to my father this oaf had money for years to drink away at the tavern.

My father had Zipporah and her mother installed as guests in our villa. The pair was astounded at the opulence of our lives, and they lunged at the delicacies on our table as if they had fasted for thirty days. But my father was right about me. Back then, my soul was a slave to the lusts of my body and the delights of my eyes. And Zipporah did indeed delight me. I stared at her like an idiot. She laughed at me, and spoke in her poor girl's coarse Yiddish about how much she loved the fine food in our house, and how she formerly had to scrape and beg for a crust of moldy black bread.

As with Carolina, I did not care what she babbled out of her mouth so long as I could indulge the base lust of my eyes and lose myself in the vision of her thick hair and curving hips. My soul had already become blackened and debauched. I still could not pay attention to a page of Talmud; but now it was because I dreamt of Zipporah lying invitingly in a valley filled with red flowers and soft grass.

All the same, my father was pleased. He was sure that, once I had married and tasted the pleasures of love with my properly Jewish wife, I would lose all interest in the Princess. Before I knew it, we were under the *chuppah*, we exchanged rings, and we had a lavish wedding feast. The Duke himself attended my wedding, although not the Duchess (and this time the Duchess kept Carolina back in the castle).

I was led to my new bed chamber, where my new wife awaited me. I was trembling in anticipation of the garden of enchantments I was about to enter. The smell of her freshly washed and perfumed body wafted to me as I entered. I dove for the bed—and then froze in terror.

Zipporah's hair was gone. Of course I knew that, like any Jewish bride, her hair would be completely shorn off on her wedding day, but it is one thing to know and another thing to see. You must remember, *Rebbe*, back then I was a slave to my eyes, and I felt nothing, and understood nothing, except what my eyes saw and felt and understood. My eyes had been besotted with Carolina's long blonde hair, and then with Zipporah's long black hair, but now her head was bare. The desire for her drained from my body. My eyes were furious in their disappointment.

Zipporah's nervous smile faded into an embarrassed glance downward at the bed cover. It is a sin, I recalled, to shame a daughter of Israel. So I entered the bed and did my husbandly duty. But while my body lay with Zipporah, my mind saw only Carolina with her long blonde hair, once again the sole delight of my wicked, straying eyes.

IV. Between Two Worlds

SO I WAS not the most satisfied of husbands. My father had tried to tempt me back to the Torah with a Jewish wife to delight my eyes, but in the end I found no pleasure in her appearance. And she was still a boorish village girl who slurped her soup and licked goose fat off her fingers. She became hateful, disgusting, in my eyes. I avoided her—I lingered at inns, I volunteered for business expeditions that would take me far away. And I eagerly continued to dine often at the Duke's table with the Princess Carolina.

Then the Wicked One devised a new snare for me. The Princess summoned me to her personal estate in the mountains in the Duchy's southwest. She had recently inherited this estate and some other property from some noble kinsman who had died—the families of those great nobles are endlessly confusing, so don't even try to ask me who this benefactor was—but anyway, she now had this property, all her own, and needed to put her financial affairs in order.

Thus I was bidden to join her household to sort out whatever needed sorting out.

You can imagine with what glee I packed my belongings and set out. My father hung his head in shame and warned me to be careful—keep to yourself, he said, try to find some Jews nearby and stay with them if you can. The Princess's household, he warned, is merely an extension of the Duchess's household, and the Duchess wished nothing but evil upon the house of Israel and me especially. But, goaded by my *yetzer hara*, my evil inclination, I was overjoyed at the chance to feast my eyes upon the Princess's beautiful form, and I was determined to linger at her manor house as long as I could.

Those first few days were the most blissful of my long time walking this Earth. The manor house was halfway up a smallish mountain draped in apple trees and pink flowers. When my wagon curved up the bend toward the veranda, there she was skipping and singing in a white linen dress, barefoot with freshly-picked pink flowers jutting out of her messy golden hair. There were giggling handmaidens all around her.

Dinner that first night should have made me flee back to my father's table. The cook served nothing but roasted pork. Everyone there watched me to see what I would do. As I knew, and they knew, my father would never touch pig meat, even at the Duke's table—that was one of his few hard rules when it came to pleasing His Excellency. They were testing me.

And my faith in the Torah, and all my years of study of the words and deeds of our holy sages, failed me. I knew I would be fated to board with a nearby family of village Jews if I refused the pork. In that Jewish home the food would be kosher, and the company pious and eager for words of Torah, but I would lose my Princess, with her lovely gold locks, for a wretched old nattering hag in a greasy horsehair wig.

So I ate the pork, although it took tremendous effort to swallow. My body felt as if it had been bathed in urine. But then, right across from me, Carolina cocked her head, ran her fingers playfully through her hair—oh that hair, may it be cursed—and smiled at me. A big, guileless smile of real affection. My shame washed away, and I was lost in the joy in which this smile now bathed me.

So I took another bite as she watched. This piece went down more easily. I started to take pleasure in the subtle and refined spices with which the meat had been seasoned.

She laughed softly. More smiles, more fingers through her hair.

Egged on by her approval, I devoured plate after plate of this filthy forbidden meat. And the more I ate, the happier she became.

I told you that I was a terrible sinner, *Tzaddik*. I see you cannot even look me in the eye right now. Well, it only gets worse. We have still not discussed my truly awful crimes.

The next day I was hard at work. The estate's affairs really were a mess, and the Princess did need my assistance quite urgently. That dead noble kinsman, whoever he was, had not paid much attention to his business concerns. The tax records were a jumble; and it was unclear exactly who owed what amount and when it fell due. The same estate privileges and lands had been leased out to multiple persons at the same time. And on and on it went.

In the early evenings, as the sun set, I left my makeshift study to join the Princess, her handmaidens and her confessor in the parlor. I would bow and provide a meticulous update on my progress and the difficulties that still lay before us. The Princess would question me further on this, that or the other point. Her questions were remarkably sharp for a girl raised in a rarefied air of otherworldly piety. She was as intelligent as she was beautiful. I worshipped her then, sinning fool that I was.

In the beginning of my stay, I would pray in the evening and in the morning, and try to study a page of Talmud each day. But something about that villa kept tempting my soul into sin. The smell of the flowers, the wafting breezes, the sweeping vista of the valley stretched below us—all these things would divert my eyes from my prayers and from the words of our sages of blessed memory. With each day, I prayed less, I studied less. The Wicked One was leading me in slow circles into the mire.

On one particularly lovely day the Princess unexpectedly interrupted me as I was working through the ledger books and old contracts. You work too hard, she chirped sweetly, you need to come outside, the weather is simply perfect.

So off we went to the rear of the villa, where there was a garden, with winding gravel paths and babbling brooks and birds full of song. We walked far off into this garden, to the point where the garden turned into forest. Carolina glowed magnificently in the broken sunlight that peeked through the leaves and branches above our heads. She wore another white dress, and a crucifix hung about her neck. Jesus, the only other Jew I had seen in so many days, gave me an anguished look. I believe even he was disgusted by my transgressions against the commands of the Torah. I tried to avoid his gaze.

The Princess directed me to sit upon a stone bench in a clearing. She looked into my eyes. My eyes shone back at hers with delight and adoration, and my heart raced. She did not smile. Her expression was intense, concentrated—as if she was searching my face for something.

Her words, when she finally spoke, were the true beginning of my downfall:

Zalman, she said, I believe you are a good man. You are honest, you are wise, you are strong. I have grown very fond of you and I have taken an interest in your welfare. I want to help you. There is something I need to speak to you about, of the upmost importance. It will not be easy for you, but I must speak the truth and try to help you while there is still time left.

Zalman, she continued, if you do not change your ways and seek salvation in the Church and embrace the truth of the Christian faith with all your heart, if you do not do these things, your soul will be lost and you will be condemned to eternal torment and suffering. This cannot be easy for you to hear, I know, you were raised in a house of errors and lies, and your father, clever as he may be about money, refuses to open his eyes to the revelation of Christianity.

At night, in my dreams, I see devils roasting your flesh in Perdition. I hear your terrible, agonized cries of pain, and I cannot help you, because it is too late to rescue your soul. Please, please, I beg you, cast off your errors. Open your eyes and see the truth.

I know you are ready to abandon the ways of your stiff-necked people. You know their stale, silly laws are empty of God's grace and love. You ate the pork I served you. At first, you were so scared. But did anything happen to you? Of course not. Our Lord is not interested in the content of your belly, He cares about the faith of your soul, the feelings of your heart.

Tell me you will accept baptism. I can protect you from any retribution from your father. The Church will not recognize the awful marriage he forced you into. You can choose to live a life of holiness in a monastery, devoted to the study of holy books, or I am sure we could find you a Christian wife.

And all this she said to me with such innocent pleading eyes. As if all would be well if I only accepted the cure for my illness, which I had been so obstinately refusing.

So what did I do?

No need to fear the worst: I was never baptized.

But, to my shame, I did not walk away either. I had never been so close to the Princess, and her presence was intoxicating. I was trembling with joy to be so near her that I felt her breath massage the tip of my nose.

So what did I do? I stalled. I told the Princess that the matters she spoke of were of the gravest importance and were not to be taken lightly. Time was needed to ponder everything.

Carolina took my hands in hers—the first time we had touched—those hands were so soft and those fingers so slender, so elegant. I tried my best to conceal my excitement.

Take the time you need, she said to me, you will not be forced. The Creator endowed us all with free will, and it is up to you to embrace the truth by your own choosing. But please remember, your very soul hangs in the balance.

The Princess never directly raised the matter of baptism again. Still, she stayed close to me, watching over me. She would sit with me while I worked away at her account ledgers. There were more walks in the garden paths. She even insisted I escort her to mass in her private chapel, where I sat on a bench while she took communion.

As I said, she did not discuss baptism again, but that does not mean we spent our time discussing chicken soup recipes and tax receipts. No, she spoke of her favorite stories of holy martyrs. She would sigh with despair at the thought that her father was going to force her into a marriage against her will, and her chastity and purity were going to be sacrificed for the Duke's worldly greed and ambition. She longed to be a virgin forever—can you believe it? Every Jewish maiden dreams of becoming a bride and a mother, but this *shikse* had mad fantasies of being an old maid in a convent.

It was clear that I had become the favorite of the Princess. Her handmaidens showed me more and more honor each day, making sure I had my favorite foods to eat and wine to drink, laundering and mending my clothes promptly, even sewing me new garments from the rarest and most refined fabrics.

I yearned for this idyll to continue forevermore: in the beautiful villa on the mountain, circled by lovely gardens and streams, living in luxury under the kind gaze of the beautiful princess with the golden hair. I had found a way to return to *Gan Eden*, living off the bounteous land with my Eve. And there were no serpents to be seen.

I did my best to extend my time at Carolina's estate. Letters flew at me from my father, my mother, my wife, my sisters, all demanding to know what had become of me and when I was returning home. These were just distractions from my beloved, so I ignored them, which of course only brought ever more urgent letters down upon my head. So I sent my father a one paragraph note about how knotted and tangled the noble lady's affairs were, such that I could not know when I would be able to return, but please give my regards to everyone and tell them to stop sending me all these letters.

Yet I knew my joy could not last. The Princess wanted an answer: Either I embrace the faith of Edom and make her happy, or I hold steadfast with the Torah and lose her affection. I was dancing atop a chasm, and soon I would need to plant my feet on one side or the other.

Much as I would like to tell you, *Rebbe*, that I never wavered from the Torah, it would be a lie. The teachings of our sages, the wisdom of my father, the bonds of our people, all felt so distant and unreal to me as Carolina lay on a nearby couch embroidering a quilt while I labored over her finances. Only she and that long mane of flaxen hair, and those grey eyes and that slight smile; only these things were real to me. I felt I could not bear to part from her. I imagined returning home to my wife, with her ugly village Yiddish, and her greasy wig and I shuddered with disgust.

But I was not so blinded by Carolina's beauty that I could not foresee certain problems. Even if I did convert, I could never marry my beloved. The Duke would only marry his daughter to another mighty nobleman. My father would consider me to be dead, and out of consideration to him, I would be dismissed from the Duke's service. So I needed some assurance the Princess would keep me in her employ. I resolved that if she would swear never to part from me, I would embrace her church and her faith.

Don't look at me like that, *Rebbe*. A Jew would think you are poised with a pistol, ready to spill blood, with a look like that on your face. I told you I had sinned greatly. Why do you think I have been avoiding the judgment that comes with death?

So on one of our walks, I told the Princess I needed to speak with her urgently. It was a late afternoon, on another perfect day, not too hot and not too cold, with a breeze just strong enough to comfort weary bones. The pink-purple light of the sunset was peaking at us from between the leaves of the trees in Her Ladyship's garden.

We sat down on a bench by a small fountain. I remember there was a little idol in the fountain, a stone angel, out of whose mouth clear, fresh water dribbled steadily. Carolina's face was shining with radiant joy, as she no doubt assumed I had finally agreed to forsake Israel for Edom.

I said I had been thinking over the profound spiritual matters, which we had previously discussed. But I was worried. All my family members were Jews. Should I abandon Israel, they would abandon me. How could I live so alone?

You need not worry, Carolina replied, I have ample estates and I will make sure you are paid a pension regularly, as my ward, so your physical needs will be attended to. I will employ you as an estate administrator. And I will insist that my mother and my future husband assist as well in your support. I will never let it be said that renouncing error and falsehood led a true Christian into poverty and dishonor.

These words were not enough to lift the heaviness from my heart. So I said, that is very generous, my lady, but my portion in this world is not merely gold and wine and fine clothes, but also the affection and love of my family and my wife. I will be all alone without them.

Our Savior will be with you, she said, He will warm your spirit when you are lonely. His grace will lift you up. And if you need an earthly helpmeet, I will let you marry any one of my servant girls.

I thanked her again, but expressed concern that a Christian wife would always look down upon me because I was born a Jew. Only the Princess, I said, truly knew my heart, and only she could ease my suffering. Could I stay, I asked, in her direct personal service forever, at her side, wherever she may roam?

Carolina now inched away from me on the bench and cast her eyes downward. She said to me: You must choose the truth because of your love of truth and His holy sacrifice on the cross and not for any other reason. Or for any other love.

I said back that I do choose truth from the love of truth. But I do not want to be tempted back into error out of loneliness.

You will not be alone. I will see to that, she replied.

But without you, I said, I am always alone, you were the one who showed me the truth, and without your beauty lighting their way, my eyes cannot see the path they should follow.

She backed away even further. There was a flash of something I had never seen before in her eyes—anger? Disgust? Whatever it was, she now spoke her words coldly and slowly: I fear, dear friend, that you see better with your eyes than you hear what I have said with my tongue. I fear you are being assaulted by the snares and traps of the Wicked One.

When I saw her start to walk away, tears flooded my eyes. Do not leave me, do not leave me, I wailed and moaned.

She looked at me then with such disappointed eyes. These tears of yours, she said, do not come from a pure source. Your heart is in the wrong place. I see that I have led you astray, when I meant only to show you our Savior's abundant love and grace. I am sorry and hope you will forgive me. You must return to your father's home tonight.

Before I could compose myself and stand up again, she had disappeared. When I arrived back at the villa after wandering listlessly through the forest by myself, I was met by a stern valet who explained that my bags had been packed and loaded onto a carriage. I was immediately escorted to that same fine carriage, shoved in and, after the gilded door slammed on my cheek, the coachman took off at a breakneck pace.

V. Vengeance

THE CARRIAGE REACHED my father's house when the sun was rising. I had not slept that night. I kept looking out the window, up at the trees and the moon and the stars feeling stunned. And numb. I constantly replayed in my mind my last conversation with the Princess Carolina, over and over again, but I was not yet able to feel sorrow or anger.

The coachman tossed my bags haphazardly upon my father's threshold, and yanked me roughly out of the carriage. Before there was time to curse the insolent wretch, he was off again. All the banging and commotion brought my mother outside. She gasped at the sight of me—my fine clothes disheveled, my eyes bloodshot from sleeplessness, dust coating me from head to toe—and brought me inside.

I fell down onto a hard wooden chair in the kitchen. Only my mother was awake. She poured me some strong brandy, which eased the tightness in my muscles. Once my body began to relax, exhaustion overcame me. The next thing I recall is waking many hours later. A doctor was anxiously examining me, and my mother and my wife were both pacing the floor behind him.

The doctor told me I had been quite ill. My forehead apparently burned like the hell fires of *Gehenna* itself. I had babbled incessantly in my delirium—of *Gan Eden*'s beautiful fountains, of the treachery of Eve in exiling me from Paradise. While the doctor thought I was looking better, it was a couple of days more until I was back on my feet.

And then my father summoned me. He was no fool, and he realized something had gone terribly wrong. His intuition was backed by the rumors he began to hear of the Princess's displeasure with me. This turned out not to be a worry for the Duke, who blamed the whole affair on the miserable, piously suffering Duchess and her conniving monks, who always plotted against His Excellency's favorite Jews.

However, the Duke's good humor was not enough to soothe my father's unease. The Duchess could regain influence at some point. Or the Duke could die—after all, even a man like him, built like an ox and then some, is not immortal. So my father needed to know what had occurred between me and Princess Carolina. Why, he asked me, did the Princess send you home so suddenly and with such dishonor?

I was ashamed before my father. He had lived his whole life around Dukes and Princesses, had seen scores of radiant *shikse* beauties paraded before him, and yet had remained a faithful member of the House of Israel. And I had nearly succumbed to an unthinkable crime, which would have poisoned his remaining years, simply out of lust for one pretty gentile girl. Why was she so exalted? In the World to Come she will not be worthy of the scraps from the tables of the holy sages studying at the Celestial Academy. When the Messiah comes—may it be speedily and in our days, amen—she will not merit living in the Holy Land of Israel, she will never hear the Levites' beautiful songs in the restored Temple in Jerusalem. So how could I have abased myself so shamefully before what was, in truth, a lowly creature, even if, in this world of shadow and illusion, she played the part of a beautiful princess with golden hair?

So I stared at my feet, and I sighed, but I could not answer my father. What happened? he pressed me. I must know. No matter what your crime, Zalman, we can figure out what to do. But I must know everything.

I remained silent, and still could not look him in the eye.

My father rose, and walked slowly towards me, letting me hear his heavy boots bang upon the ground. He stood over me. I started to sob and moan. After a few moments of letting me wail like a small boy, his hand smacked me so hard across the face that I fell over.

That brought me to my senses. I had to say something, so I said as much of the truth as I could. I described how initially I had been treated with great honor and respect, how much I had done to sort out Her Ladyship's affairs, but that she had unsuccessfully tried to convert me to her faith and to lure me away from Israel.

My father looked down, stroking his thick beard. I could not tell whether he believed me.

So, he asked me, I take it you refused? Otherwise, you would be there and not here.

I nodded.

But there was nothing else you did to make the Princess displeased with your conduct?

No, nothing, I insisted.

He stroked his beard some more, and started to pace about the room.

The Duke, he went on, will not appreciate her conduct. His Excellency values his Jewish subjects and does not want them harassed. Still, you should not be seen or heard from at the Duke's court for a while. You and Zipporah shall travel to your uncle, on the other side of the Duchy. He leases His Excellency's distilleries there. You should know something of that trade, too. Go there until after Sukkoth, and when you return here matters will have calmed down. I am hopeful to have arranged the Princess's match to a neighboring Prince by then, so she will be thankfully shipped out to another land.

He paused and sighed, before continuing:

Your mother yearns for the blessing of a grandchild to be a comfort in her old age. It would be a fitting show of your love and devotion to Israel if you could, while away, take to heart the *mitzvah* of bearing sons and daughters for the future of Israel.

And before I knew it, I was with Zipporah at my uncle Mordkhe's distillery. Mordkhe and his Devorah were kindly souls, lovely, simple Jews who prayed joyously to their Creator and fretted over the production of their brandy. Mordkhe himself never drank a drop of liquor, which was how he had won the right to operate the Duke's alcohol monopoly—the Duke swore he was the only man in the whole Duchy to be trusted not to steal any of His Lordship's excellent goods. The distillery was next to an inn they also leased from His Excellency, where Mordkhe gave Zipporah and me the use of one of the back rooms.

This should have been an opportunity for me to recover my spirits and regain my bearings. By day, I studied all the details of the liquor business. By night, I lay with Zipporah and—may all Israel be so blessed—she was soon with child. I even grew fond of my wife. Although I had been unkind to her, she remained kind to me, always tending to my needs. She was in awe of my learning, and would ask me questions about the teachings of our holy sages. I purchased some books in Yiddish for her, which she could read and which helped to satisfy her appetite for knowledge. While she had been reared in the gutter and the swamp, she turned out to be a fine flower.

I see a smile starting to sneak across your face, *Rebbe*. You are thinking you have heard the worst of it, and I am a man whom you could defend before the Heavenly Tribunal. But do not rush so fast to a lenient judgment. You have not heard the worst yet.

So, as I said, this should have been the time when I turned away from the sins of youth and returned to the pious ways of my childhood. Yet it was not to be. For while I acted the good Jew, my heart seethed in silent torment.

In those first days at Mordkhe's inn, I longed for the Princess. When I lay with Zipporah I closed my eyes and saw Carolina's golden locks and swaying hips, I heard her gently bubbling, clear laughter. The world still felt so empty being far away from the Princess. I did not long for the presence of the *Shekhinah*, I longed instead for this *shikse*.

But as one day faded into the next, and days piled up into weeks, my grief turned to anger. I said to myself, she must have known of my love for her all along and tried to use it to lure me into apostasy. She paraded her body immodestly before my eyes so that I would be led astray from my wife, who covered herself up like a decent Jewish woman. Why would the Princess do this? To hurt me, to guarantee the damnation of my soul for betraying Israel. And I had almost succumbed.

I saw the Princess now in the blackest terms. No doubt, she would prey upon other Jews with the same temptations she had used with me. That beautiful hair, those eyes and hips and legs would be used again and again as a snare to entrap unwitting honest Jews. I had to do something. Not out of revenge, I told myself, no, that would be a base motive, but rather as a champion of the sons of Torah who needed to be protected from her tricks and wiles.

But what to do? The Princess was powerful, and my father served her father, a great lord. Ordinary means of resistance—the means we employ in our everyday struggles in the light of day—would be no avail. I needed to rob Carolina of the power she wielded from her beauty, and I had to do so secretly and from a distance. She must be cursed, afflicted with hideous boils, I swore, but I did not know then the magic to make this happen.

So what could I do? Back to the beginning, I thought: it was time to study. My spare time was soon devoted to poring over books of esoteric knowledge. After exhausting the nearby library, I traveled around the Jewish communities of the Holy Roman Empire in search of ever rarer books, convinced that hidden somewhere was the masterwork that would reveal all.

While many mysteries were revealed to me, nowhere did I uncover the solution I was seeking. All the books I found showed the way to ascend to ever greater communion with the Throne of Glory. Yet I craved the terrible power of heaven to be my own, so that I could wield it here down below against my adversary, the Princess.

These books would no doubt have served you well, *Rebbe*. For all I know you have read them. They were good guides for *tzaddikim*. But I was not a would-be saint. I yearned to be a vengeful, mighty sorcerer.

My obsession consumed my soul. I slept little, and read too long by dim candlelight. My eyes weakened, surrounded now by puffy balls of inflamed purplish skin, and I spoke cruelly and impatiently to my Zipporah. Our baby was born, a little boy named Yehezkel after my grandfather of blessed memory, but I paid him no heed. What use was an infant to me? I had to save the men of Israel from the hideous temptress somehow. If anything, the thought of my son and how the Princess could one day twist him as she had twisted me caused me to redouble my efforts.

Once I was in a distant city. The pretext for the trip was to consider purchasing something or other, but the true reason was that the town's *bet midrash* was famed for possessing a cache of manuscripts by a scholar who supposedly had penetrated deeper into the holy mysteries than any other scholar of his generation.

I arrived in the town around noontime. The day was filled with my anxious playacting as I pretended to be concerned with business, lodgings, prayers, when I would gladly have slept in a ditch and filled my belly with mud just so long as my eyes could feast on those manuscripts.

After evening prayers, I went straight to the *bet midrash*. The town's leading citizens peaked through the windows at me and pointed me out to their sons—look, there, that is a real pious Jew! No drinking in the tavern for him, he makes straight for a tractate of the Talmud when he travels to faraway lands.

Yet these were no Talmud tractates in my hands. I studied feverishly. The sun set, the candles dimmed, the old men who had been studying shuffled home and still I ploughed on through the mystical texts. Great visions would start to form in my head, but then break up into scattered drops of mist. The truth was close, until it would jump away from my grasp.

The street outside was deathly quiet. The only other man there with me, the fat beadle, was snoring loudly. My body trembled as I read on. Some of the candles burned out, but I was too enraptured to attend to the ever dwindling light in the room. The letters began to swim and jumble before my eyes, and so much sweat fell from my forehead that I could barely see the text before me. The sweat soon mingled with tears of bitter frustration.

And then something extraordinary happened. Into the *bet midrash* walked a bent old Jew, barely bigger than a boy, with a white scraggly beard that fell to his waist. He wore big boots with a loud stomping heel that somehow did not wake the snoring beadle.

The strange little man sat down on the bench next to me.

Zalman, he said, why are you so troubled?

You may be wondering—how did he know my name? Had I met him before? In truth, he was a complete stranger. But I lacked the strength to think clearly at the time, so I took it as perfectly expected that this old man would wander into the *bet midrash* after midnight and know my name.

So I said to him: The truth is here, in these texts, I know it, yet it eludes me.

He said back to me: What truth are you looking for? I have read these books many times, and maybe I even helped to write some of them. There are many truths in them, like winding and intersecting paths among caves deep inside a mountain.

So I told him what I needed—the power to fell Carolina's beauty, to curse her, so she could no longer use immodest displays of her flesh to lure fine Jews into apostasy and sin.

But wouldn't it be better, the little man said, to acquire the power to elevate the souls of the men of Israel, so that their lustful eyes would not lead them astray? She would be harmless then. And the so-called great lords and ladies of this world of illusion are to be pitied anyway, as their shock will be devastating when they enter the World to Come and discover the actual lowly status of their sordid souls.

I held my ground. The Princess was too powerful, too beautiful, and the men of Israel were too weak.

The little man sighed mournfully, and scolded me for crediting too much the false idols of the flesh that had entranced my foolish eyes. If you insist, he said to me, on delving into these realms, then you should know that these holy texts cannot help you. The truth eludes you because, as you reach out and ascend, the angels attending the Throne of Glory can see into your soul, and they see what you desire, and so your wits are scattered and fail you. For what you wish, you need to consult a very particular teacher. Leave this town tomorrow, take the main road out heading west, and travel up into the nearest mountain. Ask around the villages on the mountain's bottom for Joseph the Healer. He can help you.

The next thing I recall was being poked in the ribs by the well-rested, yawning beadle. I had fallen asleep on a bench, covered in a pile of crumpled yellow pages, and it was now time for morning prayers. I prayed as best I could, went back to the inn to gather my belongings and settle accounts, and then set out in a hired coach.

I slept through the beginning parts of the trip, and awoke to a stupendous vision: on either side of the carriage were beautiful golden fields rustling merrily in the breeze, and right in front of me was the incline of the mountain. The bottom rung of the mountain consisted of villages of thatched huts and bushes exploding with brightly colored berries and flowers. But just above them nothing was visible except a grey fog. I could not even see where the top of the mountain was, so dense was this mist.

I told the coachman to drive into the village, where we would stop to water the horses and get ourselves some re-freshment. The coachman asked me where exactly I was heading. He had never been on this mountain, as the people nearby were convinced it was cursed. I told him not to worry, I just needed directions from the villagers. That silenced him for the moment.

The carriage drove through the dirt roads and alleys amongst the huts and rundown chapels until we found an inn. The coachman led the horses to the stable, while I went inside, found myself a table, and ordered a bowl of soup and a hunk of black bread.

Once my belly was full, I asked the innkeeper where I could find Joseph the Healer. The innkeeper came closer and looked me over head to toe, scratched his chin and mumbled something such as he looks fine, why does he need the Healer. So I said it was on behalf of my sick child that I had traveled to this place, in search of healing.

The innkeeper nodded and said, Go past the monastery further up the mountainside, turn left until you reach a gigantic rock covered in thick green moss, and wait there—the Healer will show his face soon enough. I thanked him graciously and called down blessings upon his head for his aid in helping an innocent child.

It was not much longer before the carriage was moving again and we had reached the monastery. To the left we could see nothing but thick grey mist. The coachman refused to go any farther. Those lands are cursed, he insisted, and he was going to stay right where he was, under the protection of the holy monks whose prayers and sacred relics no doubt kept the evil in the mist at bay.

I was irritated, but what can one do with an unwilling horse? Better to walk, so walk I did. I left my coachman behind and stepped into the mist. I could see the dirt road at my feet and follow its turns, but above my head and to each side were nothing but fog. The air smelled heavy and damp, like a swamp. After a while my stomach turned in a bad way, and I vomited up the inn's soup and bread. Still, so close to my goal, I forced myself forward.

The road ended when I reached an immense boulder covered in horribly stinking green moss. There were large beetles crawling in every direction on the rock, and occasionally entering into vicious combat. The creatures emitted faint sounds, not gentle buzzing sounds but enraged, embittered hisses.

I did not care about these ill omens. I sought only one thing, and so I called out loudly, Joseph the Healer, I have come to seek you and your wisdom.

A deep, booming voice answered: You sought and you have found, good Jew.

Where are you? Show your face.

Then out of the mist stepped a tall, strapping man in lovely moon-colored silk robes. His face shone brightly like a star, and he smelled of incense and delicate spices. This Joseph led me to the other side of the rock, where there was a tiny, rickety hut. The structure was so flimsy it would have barely qualified as a *sukkah*. I could not imagine how it could contain such a huge, strong man, much less store his silks and his perfumes.

But once we passed the threshold, inside I beheld an immense palace of such luxury and wealth as cannot be conceived. Remember, I was no fool of a village Jew. I was a merchant to dukes and princesses. I knew a thing or two about great lords and their palaces. Yet this was something beyond my wildest fantasies. The floors, ceilings, and walls were all made from white marble, and the furniture was inlaid with gold or precious jewels. Everything was radiantly lit even though I could see no candles or torches.

Joseph led me through a series of winding rooms and hallways—the enormity of the hidden palace was astounding—until we reached a library room. In the middle of the room were two chairs covered in red cushions. Joseph sat in one and motioned me to sit in the other.

He spoke to me: Zalman, I know who you are, why you are here and who has sent you to me. I know you are not here for healing. You are no fool peasant. You are a deeply learned Jew who has seen into profound mysteries. So let us speak openly about what you want and what the price shall be.

I took in stride his knowledge of things I had not said, including my name. After all, I had been led here by a being who was clearly not bound to this lower realm. So I responded with equal frankness: You are right, Joseph, I do not seek healing. There is a wicked princess who uses her great beauty to lure pious young Torah scholars to sin and heresy. I seek a spell to destroy her beauty, so she can do no more harm to the holy community of Israel.

That is dark knowledge, he said, but I can help you.

He then told me who he really was, to show the proof of his boast. For the so-called Joseph the Healer was none other than Joseph della Reina. I see, *Rebbe*, you turn white at the name, and well you should. The legend was true. This was the arrogant Spanish rabbi who had tried to summon the Messiah on his own to force history's end. And he came close, he had the demon monarchs Lilith and Ashmedai in chains when Lilith's pleading eyes and lips, with their tempting allure, led him astray and his soul was cursed. Now he served Lilith. He gathered souls for her through his false healing arts: He enacted magical cures, indeed, by using enchantments to take away a person's portion of bliss in the World to Come in exchange for healing their filthy bodily husks in this world. The price of the healed body was a soul shredded to bits.

But what I had asked was beyond even his powers as a sorcerer. Behind that pink marble door, he said, is a bedroom, where you will find my mistress Lilith. You must speak to her.

I was about to ask where this door was when suddenly a door appeared between the bookshelves, even though there was no such door when I had entered the room. Without further discussion through the door I went. There I found a room dimly lit by a reddish lamp. In the middle was a large bed enclosed in a canopy of thick red curtains.

A voice, sweet as a nightingale, called to me: Zalman, dear, come to bed. Let me see you.

I blindly obeyed, as though I were walking in a dream. Once the curtains were parted, there she was, Lilith, in a pink silk nightgown that left her legs and neck exposed. Her form was lovelier than any human woman's form could ever be—even Princess Carolina could not delight the eyes as Lilith did. Her hair and lips were crimson and her eyes were black, but her skin was like white marble. She told me to lie down next to her. Once more I obeyed, although I kept all my clothes on my body.

She stroked my cheek and nestled up to me so that her breath—which smelled of the most fragrant flowers—fell heavily upon my face. I trembled with desire. What ails you, Zalman? she asked. How can I soothe your pain? Has a wicked woman broken your heart?

My heart is whole, I said, still shaking. I dearly love my wife, a fine daughter of Israel.

Of course you do, Lilith said softly. But some misfortune has led you to me. I can see that. Speak openly, let me help you.

So I told her what I wanted: an end, forever, to Carolina's bewitching beauty.

Lilith smiled tenderly. Dearest Zalman, she replied, the merit of your study of the Torah for so many years has earned you an ample portion in the World to Come. You will have to surrender that portion to me, in full, in order to achieve your heart's desire.

I swore I would do so.

Then you must lay with me, here, in this bed, to seal our pact.

And so I disrobed and lay with the demon Lilith. Now you see, *Rebbe*, how great are my sins? You are already quaking in your chair, holy *tzaddik*, but the tale is not finished.

VI. The Curse of Leprosy

I AWOKE BACK on the road, right outside the monastery walls. I had no idea how I had returned to that place, but my body did not feel stiff or pained, so I could not have been lying there long. After dusting off, I knocked at the monastery gates, asked after my coach and driver, and soon enough I was returning to my home. On the journey back I observed nothing and thought nothing; I was like a mute beast of burden being dragged along on a tether.

You may wonder: Did I feel any desire to repent then? I had, after all, dallied with Lilith herself and squandered the reward for my years of Torah study. But there were no such thoughts in my mind. Nor was there any feeling of satisfaction at finally achieving my goal.

I eventually reached my father's house (our time with Uncle Mordkhe having run its course). The coachman bolted as soon as he received his fee, no doubt relieved to be rid of me. Once home, I slept. And I do not mean normal human sleep, but the long slumber of a dumb beast. I must have slept two days. You, *Rebbe*, no doubt think I am now going to tell of wondrous dreams of demons taunting me or righteous ancestors admonishing me. But you are wrong. I had no dreams, only bubbling warm liquid in my belly and thick phlegm in my chest.

When this dreamless sleep ended, my soul awoke once more and thoughts began to form again in my mind. I laughed at myself. I was sure I had dreamt the encounter with Lilith, or perhaps Joseph the Healer was a fraud who had worked with—his wife? Daughter? Servant girl?—to trick and defraud me. No doubt they had robbed me. Serves me right, I thought, chasing after black magic. I had escaped the Princess's clutches, to remain an upright member of the holy community of Israel. What had I been doing running all over the countryside and neglecting my fine, honest Jewish wife?

I now attended to my Zipporah faithfully and lovingly. I would watch her doing her chores around the house and praise her skills as a housekeeper to the skies and beyond. So many praises for her beauty burst forth from my mouth that she could only stammer and blush. And soon enough more blessings came, as Zipporah was pregnant again.

I became fascinated with my little son Yehezkel. I liked to sit with him, by the window in the parlor of my father's house. I would prop him up on my lap and point out the trees and the birds to him, and tell him their names in the holy tongue. Sometimes he would smile and clap at a particularly pretty bird and my heart would fill with warmth.

But even more than my newfound regard for my family, I returned to the Torah. I studied a page of Talmud each day. Although it was surprisingly rough going—something had sapped my strength for study—perhaps I was no longer accustomed to such strenuous labor? I prayed regularly and passionately in the *bet midrash* in the neighboring village. The village Jews often begged me to chant the weekly Torah portion for them, and I always obliged.

And I turned on my father. It was not long before he had to call again on His Excellency the Duke. I boiled over with fury. How could you, I thundered, how could you travel to that hideous boor and eat the filthy forbidden food at his table? How could you sacrifice your share in the World to Come for the illusions of wealth and power in this stinking rotten world of lies and falsity? Repent, I shouted, repent now before the avenging angels descend upon your corpse with scorching iron rods! Leave the Duke to stew in his filth, stay with me and let us study the holy books together.

My father shook his head sadly and asked: What has come over you? Do you think we are commanded to be beggars and to tempt the wrath of powerful lords? If you are so disgusted by the crumbs from the Duke's table, then leave this place—everything here was built from such crumbs. Go off, wander, beg, far be it from me to hold you back from the many delights of poverty, hunger, and disease. And off he went, not so much angered by my hectoring as baffled.

Two weeks later my father returned home with startling news from the Duke's court. The son of the Holy Roman Emperor himself had been staying as the Duke's guest and as the Princess's prospective bridegroom. My father had been summoned to assist in the final betrothal negotiations. The Duke was overjoyed at his good fortune, both because his prospective son-in-law was from such an illustrious lineage and because the would-be groom made a superb hunting companion—it is a miracle any deer in the Duchy survived these drawn-out engagement discussions. Everything for which the Duke and my father had schemed together was almost in their grasp.

But then, shortly after my father had arrived at court, Carolina awoke one morning with two pale bumps on her forehead. No one thought anything of this at first, but then the bumps multiplied until they spread across her forehead, down her cheeks, on her lips, and even onto her left eyelid, leaving her left eye myopic and bloodshot. Her nose collapsed in on itself, buried under a heap of the rampaging bumps and folds and wrinkles.

The Duke's court panicked. Carolina was shut away and access to her closely guarded. They put it about that she had a slight chill on the lungs, but nothing too serious. The Duke's physician was summoned, and he knew right away what had happened: The Princess had been afflicted with leprosy. Only my father knew the diagnosis initially, and he took it upon himself to tell the Duke. This was a bad idea: The Duke beat both my father and the doctor mercilessly— my father later showed us the rivulets of welts meandering along his back where he had been whipped. Yet when the Duke at last saw his daughter again, half-blind and covered in hideous bulbous sores across her face and chest and arms, he knew the truth.

So the wedding was off. The Duke and the Duchess traded accusations. The Duke claimed one of his estranged wife's priests had resorted to black magic to curse him, while the Duchess insisted her daughter was suffering for the

Duke's endless sins of the flesh. My father just sighed sadly, and shook his head. What a pity, he said, such a beautiful girl, such opportunity for His Excellency. But our fate is not in our hands. The Righteous Judge doles out punishment and reward as He sees fit.

I felt sick to my stomach at this news. I had been lying to myself—it was true, all of it—I had lain with the demon queen Lilith and sold my portion in the World to Come in order to afflict and curse the Princess. What had I done? Was Carolina so awful? Ignorant of the truth of the Torah to be sure, but what could one expect from a daughter of Edom raised to revere their lies and idols?

I could not sleep that night. I closed my eyes, and there was beautiful Carolina in my dreams, only now hideously deformed. The sight was so awful that I was jolted awake. I wandered the house and stared out the windows at the cold stars until sleep overcame me again. But then I saw Lilith acting wantonly and shamelessly to arouse my animal lusts. And once she had driven me so mad in this dream that I begged for her favors, she showed me the tortures of *Gehenna*, of Hell, horrible sights, demons scraping the flesh off sinners with burning knives, or immersing them into cauldrons of liquid fire.

Lilith smiled, revealing the hideous fangs between her voluptuous red lips. You are coming here soon, dear lover, she cooed at me, you have no good deeds left in your account ledger to present to the Heavenly Tribunal when it comes time for your soul to be tried. You have traded them all to me. And I delivered my end of our bargain.

I awoke once more to escape these terrifying dreams. And so I passed that sleepless night, and the sleepless nights that followed.

Yet this was nothing compared to the shame I felt when I entered the *bet midrash* again to pray. The letters in the holy books seemed to smolder with rage and disgust at being held in such filthy hands. The eyes of the men around me somehow knew my secret. No unkind words crossed the thresholds of the mouths around me, but those eyes, they somehow suddenly saw the soiled rags in which my soul was now clothed.

There was no refuge—only harsh justice, everywhere. Sweat poured out of me, even though the air was cold in the *bet midrash*. My eyes turned away, towards the window—and there she was, in the street, Lilith, dressed as if she was a Christian nobleman's wife, but I knew it was her. She looked back at me with a smirk of triumph. I could not look away. I hated Lilith at that moment, hated her the way I should have all along, but I also desired her, even more than Carolina. Lilith's figure was so pleasing to the eyes.

I had traveled far down the path of sin, *rebbe*. You are not facing some poor housewife terrified she served an unkosher chicken to her dear *schlemiel* of a tailor. The blots on my soul are not little black dots, but buckets of burnt tar.

Eventually Lilith grew bored of me and walked away. I looked up at the bare wooden ceiling, and felt my feet give way. My body pounded against the floor, and everything went dark. I woke much later in my bed at my father's house.

I was bedridden for a long time, days, weeks, who knows anymore exactly, but a long time. All the food they gave me was vomited right back up, to the point where I lost my appetite even though I had grown perilously weak from hunger. I survived on small sips of brandy and hard crumbs of stale black bread.

There was no doubt in my mind that the end was near. In the half-light that peered through the blinds—a sort of never-ending twilight dimness—I could see an outline of a hulking man in a black hood, holding a long, curved sword, hovering just past my feet at the edge of the bed. Sometimes his eyes would glow like burning coals. It was the Angel of Death, smelling a fresh victim ready for slaughter.

I moaned in terror for my fate. What could I do? If I died then, I would be summarily condemned by the Heavenly Tribunal. And why, I asked myself, should I suffer so? I had acted from the noblest of motives, to stop Carolina from using her shameless behavior and treacherous beauty to lure sons of the Torah into apostasy and lies. I had succeeded—never again could she seduce a young man away from his Jewish family. I should have been welcomed into Paradise with great honors. But no, the angels and the prophets and the sages had closed their wisdom to me, they would not help me, so they had forced me to turn to Lilith for aid in smiting the wicked Carolina. I had sacrificed myself for the sake of Israel—I was a martyr! But the hypocrites hovering about the Throne of Glory would condemn me anyway.

What to do? My newfound rage spurred my mind to action. The pact with Lilith could not be undone; she had performed what she had promised to perform and was no doubt in the right to demand the agreed-upon payment for her services. But then I turned the matter over more carefully in my mind. There were actually two problems facing me. The first was all the accumulated merit I had traded away to Lilith. Yet that was only a problem if, without such good deeds to my name, my sins would outweigh my upright acts. Nothing stopped me from earning new merits in the future by obeying the commandments of the Torah or engaging in further study. So the first problem was soluble.

The second difficulty was harder. By using evil magic to deform Carolina into a loathsome monster, I had sinned. True, I had sinned out of a righteous motive, to protect my fellow Jews from temptation, but the powers of Heaven had been closed to my scheming because clearly the Holy One had not chosen to punish her in this way. I had overstepped my bounds when I had taken it upon myself to render judgment.

Still, the Gates of Repentance are always open. But I needed to be forgiven by the person I had wronged: Princess Carolina. So I swore to seek her out, confess all, and beg her forgiveness. Even if my confession cost me my life—afflicting the body of a Duke's daughter through witchcraft was no doubt a capital crime—it would be fine if it secured my place in the World to Come.

Now I started to eat again, first larger portions of black bread, then *challah* and finally meat. My strength returned. The Angel of Death faded away from my vision. My father, my mother, my wife—all were overjoyed at my recovery.

My father had told me that Carolina had been dispatched to a remote convent in the mountains where the Mother Superior had cared for lepers many times before. I found some excuse to head in that direction, hired a carriage and was on my way. My father was suspicious and warned me not to visit the Princess. She is a horrible sight to behold, he told me, her grace is gone, she is a stooped cripple covered in lumps and sores. Her body stinks of putrid rot. Leave her in peace. Do not afflict her with memories of better days.

I promised my father not to visit her—a necessary lie. How could my father understand that my soul was balanced so precariously on the scales of the Heavenly Tribunal?

This mountain was far from my father's home, and it took my carriage several days to reach it. During the journey I prepared myself by fasting during the day and praying and studying fervently. If my eyes were open during that trip, then so was either my *siddur* or a tractate of the *Gemara*.

In the village near the convent there was a rundown inn leased by an embittered old woman, the only Jew in the area. Her husband had long ago died, and her children had made matches in other communities, so she was alone on the mountainside selling beer and stew to the Christian pilgrims. You would think she would be overjoyed to see another Jewish face and perhaps even try to ply a few words of Torah from me. But no, she greeted me with a hail of curses: Don't expect properly kosher food here, Mr. Holy Rabbi, she yelled at me, and don't expect a quiet place to pray. I want no complaints from you. You eat what I cook and sleep where I tell you or you can leave.

At another time I would have taken offense at these insults to my honor. But I had no desire to cause new strife for which I would need to seek yet more forgiveness, so I meekly thanked her for her hospitality and promised to be no trouble at all. Still, I avoided her food, having brought my own provisions, and did not accrue a new sin for eating unclean food.

I spent a sleepless night in prayer and supplication. In the hours between midnight and dawn, I could see demon shapes crawling in the corner of my room. The shadows slowly formed into bodies, the bodies of naked beautiful women—Lilith's daughters—sent to tempt me away from my mission, to prevent me from ransoming my soul. I felt more terror than lust and concentrated with perfect devotion on each letter of my prayers.

I must have been an awful spectacle to behold the next morning, since the nasty crone innkeeper recoiled in horror at the sight of my bloodshot eyes. It was an easy walk to the convent from the inn. I knocked at the gate and asked to see the Princess. The nuns were suspicious at first, for what sort of man would want to visit a leper? And was I not aware that I could catch the disease from her? I refused to leave, gave my name and begged them to tell Carolina that I had traveled a far distance to visit her. After a brief delay, I was admitted to a spare stone room, a reception area for guests, I presumed.

In walked the once mighty and graceful Princess Carolina, now bent and stooped, led by an elderly nun holding her hand. Carolina wore the full nun's habit and a thick white veil to cover her face. She and her helper sat down on the opposite bench.

In the beginning my words caught in my throat and would not come out. Carolina, however, was calm and gracious as ever, thanking me for visiting her and asking politely after my family. Recovering my presence of mind, I told her I had not come to exchange pleasantries, but that I needed her help to save my soul. Both Carolina and the old nun leaned forward at those words, as you can well imagine, *Rebbe.*

I told Carolina my whole tale from beginning to end, omitting nothing, and pleaded with her to forgive me for the horrible, unspeakable wrong I had done her. But her response was not what I had expected, not at all. She laughed gently—still that same crystal clear voice—and said she could not forgive me because I had done no wrong to forgive. I was blameless and clearly quite confused. To set my mind at ease, she promised to reveal the truth of matters to me, which showed that our Creator, and not the devil or Lilith, was driving events.

I do not recall, after all these years, every detail she spoke—and there were many—but I can tell you the broad outline of her story. She had enjoyed a happy childhood. Her father ignored her in those days, so she was raised by her saintly mother in an atmosphere of serene piety. She prayed often and read many tales of Christian saints and martyrs. Everyone in that household devoted themselves to matters of faith. All she wanted was to lead a life of holiness, to do good works and care for the poor and the sick.

Carolina's bliss was dashed when her body blossomed into womanhood. Suddenly she had become beautiful. Everywhere she went men noticed her, and looked at her, but in bad ways. She was inciting sinful thoughts, she realized, but she did not want to do this—she wanted these men to stop looking at her that way; it made her feel ashamed and guilty. But they would not stop; they circled her like hungry panting wolves, although fear of the Duke kept them at bay.

Now her father, the wretched fornicating drunk, finally noticed his daughter. He saw opportunity in her misery. The Duke ordered Carolina to be in attendance at his court and to attend his banquets and tournaments and other receptions. The Duke's servants, at his orders, dressed and primped and perfumed Carolina to flaunt her loveliness. The Princess was then dangled before a very select group of wolves, wealthy, powerful noble suitors. She shuddered when she saw their eyes look her up and down and when she felt their hot breaths near her.

Carolina was distraught. Instead of a life of chastity and good deeds, she was to be the plaything of some brutal lord's most terrible, sinful lusts. Her father was forcing her to arouse these lusts by parading her about his banquet tables. She had become Satan's handmaiden and saw no way out of the devil's hideous trap.

And then it came to her: She must sacrifice her physical beauty so that the true beauty of her soul could shine forth. Heaven was testing her, she concluded, by making her so lovely and giving her so many admirers. She would not succumb to these temptations and prayed fervently, madly, for her beauty to end.

Her Savior, in His infinite mercy and goodness, pitied her and heard her prayers. When she awoke with the first sores on her face, she shed tears of joy and thanksgiving. As the sores and lumps rampaged across her face and body, she trembled with excitement and gratitude. Heaven had accepted the sacrifice of her beauty and her worldly glory. Once her father realized she was beyond cure, he quickly dispatched her to this convent.

And then—this I shall never forget—the Princess said to me, I know my former beauty bewitched you and led your soul down paths it should not have strayed. I must cure you of the harm I inadvertently did before. So, now, look closely at the vanity and illusion of the beauty of the flesh.

She pulled her veil off. The sight I beheld was monstrous: Her face was unrecognizable, there were white scaly sores everywhere; even her lips were covered. One of her eyes was overrun by the hideous lumps and appeared lifeless. The other eye was weak and fluttering. Her nose was gone—it appeared to have collapsed into her face. Most of her hair—that lovely golden hair—had fallen out, leaving only a few dry stiff strands of white hair dangling down her diseased cheek.

I looked away.

Look at me, Zalman, the Princess pleaded, look at the truth of human flesh. See how your eyes deceived you in the past. You don't need forgiveness. You need guidance, you need help to see past these illusions and snares scattered by the devil so your soul can accept the truth of Our Savior's gospel.

Words failed me. Eventually I managed to thank the Princess for receiving me, wished her well and left for home. It took me many days to recover from that horrible image. But when I did, I laughed. That is right, *Rebbe*, I laughed at the idea of repentance. How could I repent if I could not convince the wronged party that I had sinned against her, even after I had confessed everything? And how did I know I had sinned? Maybe it was fated that Lilith would be unwittingly used to answer the Princess's prayers. In my helpless confusion, I did nothing but laugh.

The Princess, if you are curious, lived out her days in that convent. She tended to the poor and the sick, when she was not praying, and became a famous holy woman. Her bones are now sacred relics, and pilgrims travel from far away to beseech them and their healing power. I imagine she has a fine seat in the Christian Paradise.

VII. The Dybbuk

AS FOR ME, I put one foot in front of the other and let my troubles slip away from my mind. I sired more children with my Zipporah. Business thrived. A partnership opportunity arose with a cousin in a large city farther to the east, so I moved there with my family. Everything was going well for me: Each venture was blessed with success, my children were healthy, my daughters lovely and my sons learned. I struck fine matches for all my children. If your *yiches* is sufficiently distinguished, *Rebbe*, I may be your ancestor, so splendid were the matches I made with the finest rabbinical families.

Nor was I stingy with my wealth. I paid for lavish renovations to the synagogue and the *bet midrash*. I supported many widows and orphans, and provided dowries to poor brides. Indigent scholars traveled to me. I fed them liberally at my table and supported their upkeep. I was growing old and fat and felt certain that, after living my fully allotted one hundred and twenty years, I would be gently guided to a pearl-encrusted golden throne in Paradise.

At least that is how I felt before the *dybbuk* came. It all started on a Friday night, after *Shabbat* dinner. As the night was mild, I was sitting on my porch sipping a wonderful tumbler of brandy. One of my sons-in-law was next to me, belaboring some obscure point of Torah, yet I paid him little mind, just occasionally giving him an encouraging word.

But then suddenly, from a house across the street, came wild screams, inhuman screams, like a monstrous beast was being slaughtered in Reb Dovid's bedroom. Jews from all around swarmed upon Dovid's house, my son-in-law among them. My wife and daughters, too, ran over there. As for me, I figured there was no more room in that house to gawk at whatever they were all gawking at and that someone would tell me the tale soon enough.

The next morning, as we made ready to walk to the synagogue, my son-in-law told me of the marvels he had seen at Reb Dovid's the night before. This Reb Dovid had a daughter, thirteen years old, named Malke. It was Malke who had been screaming. Her parents had tied her to her bed to stop her from scratching her eyes out. My son-in-law recounted how everyone in the town had pressed into Malke's room, packed in so close you could hardly breathe, and she had stared back at them all with the crazed eyes of a rabid dog.

For a long time no one spoke—not Malke, not Dovid, not anyone from the town. But Malke kept up her screaming. Until abruptly she stopped (I myself must have been asleep by then). And then Malke spoke. But it was not Malke's nervous, high-pitched voice that came forth from her mouth, but the deep bass of a grown man. The voice, speaking through Malke, asked everyone what they wanted and why they could not leave Malke alone.

Dovid replied that everyone was worried about Malke's health, and he asked Malke why her voice had changed.

Don't worry about Malke. She is unharmed for now, the voice said back.

Dovid now started to panic: Who are you? Where is my Malke?

The voice said it was not going to tell its name, but if Dovid wanted Malke left unharmed, he should clear out and take all this riffraff with him.

So everyone left. That following Saturday morning, my son-in-law, Dovid, and a few others converged on our rabbi—who, like me, had slept through the ruckus—and told him the tale. The rabbi furrowed his brow and nodded gravely several times. Later that afternoon, the rabbi went to Malke, flanked by several men, including, again, my son-in-law. I continued to stay home. After my past experience with Lilith, I was not interested in any more other-worldly wonders.

My son-in-law returned home shaking with terror. After I steadied him with some brandy, he told me his tale: When they came upon Malke she was lying perfectly still in her bed. Her eyes were wide open and unblinking, as if they were made from glass. The rabbi approached, but she did not re-act. He leaned close to her and asked, ever so gently, whether she was feeling ill, perhaps she would like some fresh cool goat's milk?

Malke's head turned to the rabbi, her mouth opened, but instead of words, she spat out a torrent of blood on the rabbi's face. Then Malke laughed, but the voice was again not her voice. *Gut Shabbos*, the voice cackled in mockery.

The rabbi stepped back and demanded to know the spirit's name and why it was seeking refuge in Malke's body. The spirit refused to answer.

So the rabbi began a series of rituals. He and the *minyan* of men with him prayed fervently, but to no avail. The rabbi uttered mysterious and esoteric combinations of holy names, but this also made no impact. The spirit laughed cruelly and made all sorts of insolent remarks.

Finally, the rabbi, frustrated and exhausted, demanded to know how the spirit could have such enormous strength as to resist such powerful prayers.

The spirit replied: The words of hypocrites are powerless against me. You shelter a great sinner, indeed, you heap honors upon this great sinner. His presence gives me power.

Is the sinner here, amongst us now? the rabbi asked.

No, and he has been careful to stay away from me, clever man that he is. I have seen many faces through Malke's eyes, but not this face.

The search was now on, my son-in-law said, for any man who had not yet visited Malke. Have you visited her? he asked me. Without thinking I said no and thus placed myself onto the list being assembled. In the end there were twenty of us, and we were ordered to parade ourselves before Malke that night, after the end of the Sabbath.

I felt a sense of dread at this exercise, but what could I do? To resist would be to announce myself as the guilty man. So I went along.

The rabbi directed us to line up outside Malke's door. We went in one at a time. Several men entered before me, and exited quickly. I could hear the spirit snicker. Then it was my turn.

I walked into this cramped little room, really nothing more than an alcove with a cot. Malke lay there with her hands and her feet tied up, writhing and turning. Her nightgown was in tatters and stank of urine. The rabbi turned to Malke: *Nu*, he said, is this the one or not?

Malke ignored the rabbi, and her feral eyes bore into me. Soon a smile crossed her lips, a conspiratorial smile. And then a chuckle.

A man's voice addressed me from Malke's body: Brother in sin, it is good to see you in the flesh, looking so plump and rich.

I felt faint and moved to leave, but the rabbi stopped me. He turned to Malke: Spirit, I have brought you the man you wanted. Now tell me your name.

It is Itzik, the spirit replied, and I was once a fine blacksmith.

So the rabbi asked: Why are you cursed to wander the Earth like this, Itzik?

And the spirit replied he had been cursed for his many sins. He had lusted after another man's wife. When his prayers for relief from this agony went unanswered, and the itching torment in his flesh grew worse by the day, he contrived ruse upon ruse to be in this lady's presence, thinking that either seeing her would soothe his ache or he would grow to find her ugly from too much familiarity. But matters only became worse. His nights were spent sweating and tossing in his filthy, sinful dreams. His own wife he ignored, for she seemed so bent and wrinkled compared to the object of his lust.

Finally, this Itzik went to a gentile woman who lived in a hut in the forest, a witch whom the Christian priests had hounded out of normal human society. After being well paid, the witch cast some spell or other and gave him a vial of something rancid to drink. Itzik gulped it down in one go. Then everything went black before him. In his dream he met Lilith, queen of the demons, who lay with him and showed him the secret magic herbs to use to seduce his neighbor's wife.

Itzik said he awoke back in his own bed. He gathered the herbs and smeared them all over his body. And soon enough, his neighbor's wife fell madly in love with him, and Itzik sated his lust. But he grew bored with just this one illicit, sinful love. His eyes wandered to a new young wife, the same herbs were applied and she was his too. And so on and on it went with all the women in Itzik's town throughout his long life. Although he had no children through his own wife, whom he neglected and scorned to the end, his lovers bore him many secret bastards.

Itzik died an unrepentant sinner. His last thoughts in this world, as the strength ebbed from his body, were of his favorite trysts and conquests. He wondered if he would be reunited with these lovers in *Gehenna*, where they could all start up again.

Yet it was not to be. Once his soul had departed from his body he found himself surrounded by avenging angels. They hacked at him with burning swords and beat him with their fists. Itzik fled. The angels chased him hard, and whenever he paused out of weariness, they would pounce upon him and begin their tortures anew. Eventually he fled to our town and made his way into a chicken. The chicken was slaughtered, and after Malke ate its meat, Itzik's spirit entered into her. And he had no desire to leave. Malke turned out to be quite a safe refuge from avenging angels.

After hearing this tale through, the rabbi scolded him for his terrible deeds, but then asked why he would slander a fine, upstanding Jew like me, a pillar of our community.

Itzik roared with laughter. He said to the rabbi: Fine, upstanding Jew? You are a fool. This Zalman has lain with Lilith, too, I can see the marks her nails made scratching his soul. He is her eternal servant as much as I am. Lilith loves nothing better than a hypocrite—someone to confuse the lines between the wicked and the just. You are damned, my brother in sin, and you and I shall both be the sport of the avenging angels and their fiery blades.

The rabbi rained curses upon the spirit's head and apologized to me for being subjected to such vicious and unfounded insults. He told me to go home.

I could not sleep that night. Was I damned? True, I had lain with Lilith, and I had afflicted an innocent girl with the curse of leprosy. But it was all so long ago, and, unlike Itzik, I had repented and turned to an upright life. I should be confident in my chances before the Heavenly Tribunal. The celestial judges would see the scales of good and wicked deeds tip in favor of my salvation, and I would be admitted to Paradise.

Yet could I really be sure? How could Itzik have seen my sins so clearly, have smelled the residue of Lilith's perfume upon my soul, if I had truly overcome my wicked deeds? Maybe my prayers had been rejected? How could I know?

And if I were wrong, I shuddered at the tortures that would be my portion in the next world. My mind could easily picture the frothing, raging avenging angels and the hideously deformed cackling spirits with whom I would wander the Earth. For the first time, death no longer struck me as the natural exit from this world of illusion, but as a terrible danger, as the end of my peace and happiness and security. I had to find a means to evade death.

Making some excuse or other I took a trip to a nearby town with a *bet midrash* stocked with many esoteric manuscripts. I read and I searched. There were many discussions of how to cure illnesses or heal wounds, or to speak to the dead. But I could find nothing that told me how to avoid death altogether. Tears of frustration poured down my cheeks.

An old man nearby took pity on me. He asked me why I was so upset and what I was seeking with so little luck. In my despair I blurted out that I was looking for a way to evade death.

The old man rubbed his beard, stared at the ceiling and hummed something under his breath. After being lost in thought for what seemed to me like an eternity, he walked into a corner, picked up a small volume and handed it to me. Read this, he said, it may soothe your worries.

The manuscript, whose letters were a bit faded, was titled the *Chronicle of Ahimaaz*. It was a history of an illustrious Jewish family in Italy and their wondrous deeds. But the *Chronicle* also told of a man who had avoided death by sewing a parchment under his skin which had been inscribed with secret, powerful names of the Holy One, Blessed be He. As long as this parchment was under his skin, he could not die.

I wasted no time in buying paper, pen, ink, needle and thread. I broke the paper into innumerable little squares and on each I inscribed a magic name or combination of letters with esoteric power. When my pile of inscribed squares was complete, I used the needle to cut an opening in my skin and then, after the squares had been inserted underneath, to sew myself back up again. This was a long, tedious procedure, as I needed frequent breaks to prevent excessive bloodletting. Nevertheless, working methodically, I succeeded in sewing each square—more than thirty in total—under my skin.

This should have killed me—so many cuts, so much poisonous black ink mingling in my blood. Yet I felt fine, although I soon noticed certain changes in myself. I stopped feeling tired and no longer needed sleep. I was not particularly energetic; rather, sleeping had stopped being something I needed to do.

The next activity that I dropped was eating, as I did not get hungry anymore. I likewise lost the need to drink water or wine to sustain myself.

Nor was I susceptible to fits of anger. On the carriage ride home our axle split in two, leaving us stranded in the middle of a field for hours under the burning late afternoon sun. The coachman raged and cursed and argued with the serfs who were trying to fix the carriage. But somehow all this seemed irrelevant to me. I did not care about being late, because time no longer pressed upon me. There was no longer any feeling of a future, just the moment I was in, like a wooden plank drifting across an ocean.

When I arrived home, I sat on a chair in my parlor, and stared out the window. There was a gnarled old oak tree right outside our house, whose twisting branches filled me with a great calm.

My wife meanwhile had gone to the *mikveh* to bathe and purify herself. The time of her monthly impurity had ended during my trip, and she desired to lie with me. But when she called me to bed later that night, my body would not respond. This surprised me. Zipporah had remained a beautiful woman, a delight to the eyes, and normally the sight of her in her bed roused my lust almost uncontrollably. Yet now I felt merely bored.

Over the next few days Zipporah tried many clever stratagems to rouse my desire. Her body was adorned with her loveliest garments; perfumes were deftly deployed to make her scent enticing; and she lost no opportunity to remove her matron's wig to reveal her real hair underneath. Nothing helped, though. I began to find her advances bothersome—they interfered with my peaceful enjoyment of the oak tree—and I would walk away with a sigh.

Zipporah grew bitter. Like all beautiful women, she was vain. This was not her fault. All her life everyone around her had reacted to her beauty. Their eyes would see her loveliness and be terrified of losing such a sweet vision, so those eyes would force their lips to praise her and their hands and feet to help her.

So now she was furious at me for not responding to her as she expected me to. This was an affront to her dignity. She took out her rage in small ways, nagging me about this errand or that chore. Her movements were tense, as if her body were one big clenched fist waiting to land on my face.

I would leave the house to get away from my wife. Zipporah's behavior had not upset me, because I no longer felt upset about anything, but the problem was that she had got in the way of my preferred pastimes of rocking in chairs and watching the world go by. There was no thought in my mind of either reconciling with her or divorcing her. I merely wanted her to stop being in front of me.

My first attempted refuge was the *bet midrash*. I pulled out a tractate of the Talmud and decided to study again. But the words bored me. The meaning of the passage was apparent to me quite readily, almost without any effort, yet it struck me as pointless. The secrets of the world were easy to discern and utterly uninteresting.

I put the tractate down and stared out the window. This was a signal to those around me, though, that I was in the mood for conversation, and so they swooped down upon me and started hammering away at my poor ears with their complaints and gossip and petty worries. I found it strange that all these men, who were at least somewhat learned, could really feel so worried about a business rival, or be so angry at their sons for lazing about on a weekday afternoon. Eventually the din of the voices proved too much for me—the hammering on my ears was preventing me from my watching a tree through the window—and I left.

I wandered out of town to the nearby forest. It was good to walk in the woods. The trees were there for my contemplation without distraction, and the time drifted away without me noticing it. When the sky grew dark, I told myself, I should head home. It would draw unwelcome attention and more hammering in my ears if I spent the night alone in the forest.

Still, as I approached my town again, I could not bear the thought of seeing Zipporah and hearing her complaints about broken shutters or incompetent maids. At the outskirts of the town was a tavern favored by the gentile peasants in the area. I went in there. I paid for a drink out of politeness to the tavern keeper, but did not touch it. It was still early for the tavern, and the place was empty. There was a window to the side and a tree branch abutting it, so I was at peace.

The tavern filled up over time. The peasants came in, dirty, smelly, and were soon quite drunk. Then they noticed that a Jew had come into their preferred place, and they were not pleased. Angry, mocking words assailed me. I made no reaction. So the words became stronger—threats of violence. At one time I would have fled in terror, but now I found it all to be only a nuisance. So again, I made no reaction.

The peasants flew into a rage. Fists pummeled me, legs kicked me, spittle flew all over my body. They shoved me to the ground. Some drunk hit me with a stool. The tavern keeper cleared everyone away. I am sure he expected to find me bleeding and unconscious, if not dead. But there was not a bruise or cut on my body. I simply stood back up and yawned. The serfs sobered immediately and retreated in horror.

This marked the end of the life I had been leading. The *dybbuk*'s accusations had not been taken seriously—it was, after all, the ranting of a terrible sinner fleeing his righteous punishment—and, after the spirit had finally been exorcised, talk of its ravings had died down. Now everyone recalled the spirit's harsh words about me, because there was no explanation, other than dark magic, for my miraculous survival in the tavern. Zipporah egged the slanderers on with her moans over my odd behavior in the house.

I realized I had to leave. So one night I packed a few belongings in a small bag and I walked away. There was no particular destination for my journey. On and on I went until I grew bored with walking and decided to settle in a town. This time I was careful to ape the manners of the fully living men around me. I claimed to be a widower and made sure that the eyes around me saw nothing but another sad, sighing Jew.

And so since then I have wandered about from town to town. I have no idea how much time has passed because I do not care. There is no purpose to my wandering, there is no destination. I walk and walk because that is better than being chased and tortured by avenging angels with fiery swords.

Such is my tale, *Rebbe*. So tell me, can you redeem and protect my soul?

VIII. A Tale of the Hasidim from the Archives of the Institute

EVENING HAD FALLEN by the time Zalman had finished his tale. The holy *tzaddik* sighed gently, and said it was time to light the *Havdalah* candle, to end the magical time of the *Shabbat* and to return to the everyday world. Zalman followed him out of the study and did not press for an answer about the fate of his soul; centuries of wandering had taught him not to rush things.

When the pair rejoined the *rebbe*'s followers, there were all manner of whispers and questions and furtive glances. But the *rebbe* ignored them all. He conducted the *Havdalah* ceremony in his usual way and then took a walk in the warm evening air. The *tzaddik* told Zalman to return to him in four days' time.

The town buzzed and hummed with rumors about what was said between Zalman and the *rebbe* and what miracle would happen at the appointed time of their next meeting. Everyone was sure the holy saint would intercede with the higher spheres and convince them to accept Zalman's soul into Paradise. Yet both Zalman and the *rebbe* refused to discuss the matter.

On the appointed day, Zalman and the *rebbe* met privately, again in the *rebbe*'s study. Immediately afterwards, Zalman departed in a carriage the *rebbe* had ordered and was never heard from again.

Years passed. The *rebbe* eventually was called to take his place in Paradise in the World to Come. Over the following decades, he slipped from the memories of the townspeople into their legends and folktales. By then, there had been great changes in the world. The Czar was toppled in the First World War, and Poland was once again an independent nation.

In the new independent nation of Poland was the bustling metropolis of Vilna, and in Vilna there was an Institute that sought to collect and study the old stories and folkways of the Jews in the little towns in the Polish countryside. This Institute had hired a smartly dressed young man to travel through these towns and transcribe whatever folktales he could coax out of the aging country Jews.

With a satchel filled with notebooks he rode the railroad to one rundown rural station after another. At one of these decrepit depots, there was a small café serving coffee and pastries and selling Yiddish newspapers. Exhausted from a sleepless night next to a loudly quarreling family on the train, the young man eagerly drank the bitter, grimy coffee. He tried reading a newspaper, but his eyes were too tired for the small ink letters.

There were no other customers. After a time, the café owner, an old Jew, sat down next to him and asked what had brought such a sophisticated young man to such an out of the way small town. Had he returned from America to visit dying relatives one last time?

The young man explained he was from Vilna, from whence the famed Institute had sent him to travel the countryside collecting stories and legends from the local Jews. This was important work, he continued, as scholars at the finest universities intended to pour over the Institute's findings to analyze and distill the true life and beliefs of the Jewish people before modernity and assimilation had begun to corrode their community.

The café owner beamed. You are in luck, young man, he said, I have a wonderful tale to tell, a true and wondrous story from this very town where I have lived all my life. I heard it from my grandfather's lips. My grandfather lived through these events and saw them with his own eyes.

The young man hastily grabbed a notebook. The café owner began his tale:

Many years ago this town was famous for its great *rebbe*, a holy *tzaddik* who was pious and learned and could intercede directly in the higher realms. One day our *rebbe* was praying in the synagogue when he noticed a Jewish householder chanting the weekly Torah portion who kept stumbling over certain words. Listening closely, our *rebbe* realized this man was unable to say only those words that are prohibited to the lips of the dead. The *rebbe* grasped immediately that this man had used some type of powerful sorcery to avoid death. Have you ever heard the legend of how a *golem* can be brought to life by sticking a parchment with the right holy words under its clay tongue? Same sort of thing here, except with a corpse instead of a lump of clay.

The *rebbe* told the dead man to sit down and stop pretending to be one of the living. The townspeople—and certainly my grandfather, then a small boy—were terrified of this hideous apparition, but the *rebbe* had no fear. He summoned the dead man to a private meeting. The dead man confessed he had been a terrible sinner—he was an adulterer, he had coveted and seduced his neighbor's wife and sired many secret bastards. Recognizing the terrible judgment awaiting him in the next world, this sinner had sewn a parchment under his skin with esoteric holy names written on it, and such was the power of the holy names that they averted death. He begged the *rebbe* to intercede for him before the Throne of Glory.

And here is the strangest thing: the *rebbe* neither intervened to save this soul, nor cursed him for his crimes. So what did the *rebbe* do? He gave the walking corpse a ship ticket to America. Off the dead man went to America, and that was the last anyone ever heard from him. Who knows, perhaps to this day he sits in a store somewhere in New York seducing lonely young wives?

Why did the *rebbe* send him to America? For the longest time he would not say. But as he lay dying, with the Angel of Death visible at the foot of his bed, he told the secret to his son-in-law. That son-in-law told his son, who told my grandfather, as the two were friends. And this is the truth of it.

The *rebbe* wanted to help the dead man, but when he looked closely he could see the avenging angels, scores of them, circling him with their fiery swords. They were itching

 Barak A. Bassman

to punish his wicked soul, yet his bodily husk continued to protect him from their retribution. The *rebbe* looked into their eyes. They looked back at him with a hatred so deep that even that fearless holy saint was stricken with terror. He could not prevail before the Throne of Glory with such determined foes in the ranks of the angels. Nor would he use his powers to break the spell and release the soul from the puffed up corpse. How could he be responsible for delivering a Jewish soul, no matter how wretched, to such ghastly tortures?

So the *rebbe* panicked and sent the dead man packing to another continent. *Nu*, that should be a fitting tale for your Institute. The *rebbe* succumbed to cowardice. A true tale, mind you, not some silly nonsense about a perfect *tzaddik* you find in those chapbooks about the Baal Shem Tov or Levi Yitzhak.

The young man dutifully recorded this tale in his notebook. As the café owner stood up again to attend to the customers who had begun to trickle in, he marveled that these old superstitious Jews could believe such foolishness. Still, it was another piece of evidence of the traditional folk culture that needed to be documented and catalogued.

To that smartly dressed young man from the great metropolis of Vilna, the tales he collected were corpses that could be dissected but not made to walk and talk, even with the most magical amulets bearing the most esoteric and holy names. He lacked the ability to penetrate to the heart of the matter.

Other Books by Barak Bassman

Elegy of the Minotaur

Repentance: A Tale of Demons in Old Jewish Poland

King Solomon and Ashmedai: A Wisdom Tale

The Twilight of the Magical Siren: A Tale of Late Antiquity